WHERE THERE'S A WILL

Leanne Banks

A KISMET™ Romance

METEOR PUBLISHING CORPORATION
Bensalem, Pennsylvania

First Printing October 1991.

ISBN: 1-878702-62-9

Special thanks to:

Mary and Carolyn for express service.

All of the supportive people at HRBC,
especially Mina, the "cruise bath" expert.

Tony and J. C. always . . .

LEANNE BANKS

As a little girl, Leanne Banks became a fan of
romance when she first heard the story of Cinderella.
After marrying her own Prince Charming and having
a son and daughter, she turned her creative energies
toward writing. There's no shortage of story ideas
for this native Virginian. "I get my inspiration from
life," Leanne says. "There's always something new
waiting around the next corner."

ONE

"Hey, Al, hand me that wrench," a deep voice called from beneath the battered truck.

Shifting her attention from the huge construction equipment filling the garage, Chelsea Collins carefully stepped over a puddle of grease and moved closer to the voice. She didn't see anyone in the near vicinity, so she looked at the array of tools in the tool box and pleased herself immensely by identifying a wrench.

"You gonna take all day?"

She slid the wrench under the truck.

He muttered thanks, then singed the air with a curse. "I stripped the bolt. Get me another one, will you?"

Now a bolt was an entirely different matter. She gazed at the variety of sizes and shapes of bolts and shook her head in bemusement.

"Al, it's hot as Hades under here and I've got to check on that bid for the new doctors' building. All I need is the bolt."

Mildly irritated with his impatience, Chelsea answered in her slow southern drawl. "Well, Mr. Slater, if you could tell me what kind of bolt you need, I'd be happy to hand it to you."

She had barely blinked her eyes before he'd slid from beneath the truck and was standing in front of her. Chelsea's apprehension increased tenfold when she took stock of her new business partner, and she automatically took a step back.

He was tall, intimidatingly so, almost a foot taller than her own five-feet-four. Curly black hair framed a square face with a broad forehead and jutting cheekbones. His thin mouth appeared hard, and she wondered what would make him smile. Something told her it wouldn't be her.

The man before her was so compelling she was barely aware of the background noise outside the garage and the late afternoon Arizona heat. His broad shoulders and powerful chest strained against the grease stained T-shirt.

And the way his jeans fit could make a woman dizzy.

Her gaze traveled back to his face and she stared helplessly. The paradox of all that hard masculinity lay in the curly black eyelashes framing his large dark eyes.

Chelsea shifted uneasily. This was not the good ole boy she'd pictured for her father's business partner.

Controlling the urge to head for the hills, she withstood his thorough examination and found herself wishing she'd worn something that covered more of her body,

Perhaps a nun's robe.

Those deep, dark eyes took in every detail from the top of her blonde head to her red toenails. He narrowed his eyes as if he were searching for a clue to her identity.

She saw the moment the light dawned and felt uneasy at the flicker of disdain that flashed through his black eyes.

"Chelsea Collins," he said in an expressionless voice, and wondered which sin he was being punished for. He'd pretty much given up on seeing her face to face.

Not exactly the greeting she'd been hoping for, but she could cope with it. Her finishing-school charm may not have much practical use, but it came in handy in a situation like this.

Mustering her most engaging smile, she said, "I'm surprised you recognize me, Mr. Slater. I know I'm glad to finally meet you. Daddy often mentioned how fortunate he was to have you as his business partner."

Jake couldn't think of a word to say. She was prettier than any of her pictures.

She felt edgy as the silence stretched between them and pushed her long blonde hair behind her ear. "Uh, I'm sure you've heard about the will." She searched in vain for some flicker of response, but there was none.

Desperate to get through this initial awkward meeting, Chelsea felt the push from her southern upbringing to fill the silence. She shifted her leather sandals. "I can see that you're terribly busy today. Perhaps we could discuss my involvement in the business a little later."

The mention of business set off an internal alarm. She could be polite and beautiful until Christmas, but Jake didn't want her near Collins and Slater, General Contractors, Inc. He'd worked too long and hard to let some flighty blonde come in and mess it up.

"How about next week?"

Chelsea blinked. "Next week!"

"We've got a busy operation here." He shrugged. "I can't stop business just to chat."

She blinked again, distracted by the breadth of his shoulders. For a second, she resented the thin T-shirt covering his upper body, then caught herself. Now was not the time for ogling.

He'd said something about chatting. Chelsea narrowed her eyes at him. He didn't want her here, and he thought he could put her off with a little male intimidation. The patronizing attitude wasn't new to her, but that didn't mean she would accept it.

"I'm afraid next week won't do, Mr. Slater. I didn't travel across the country just to chat." She saw a flash of surprise in his eyes and continued in honeyed tones. "Since I'm going to be working here for at least the next year, I need to become familiar with the construction business. After all, I wouldn't want to make any decisions that would adversely affect our company."

Bull's-eye. His eyes gave him away. Jake was afraid she was going to ruin his business. Well, no more afraid than she was herself. But Chelsea Rae Collins had spent the last twenty-four years of her life dancing to somebody else's music, and she'd finally received a golden opportunity to make something of herself. She'd allow neither Jake's fears nor her own to interfere with her plans.

He looked displeased, but she held his gaze, sensing that if she buckled under now, her cause would be lost.

He set his wrench aside, wiped his hands on a rag, and sighed heavily. "Come this way."

She followed him into a small, neat office and slid into an ancient leather chair. Sitting behind a desk, he pulled a pack of cigarettes from a drawer. He lit one and drew deeply. Chelsea resisted the urge to pluck it from his lips, but her expression must have revealed her distaste.

He raised a dark eyebrow. "Do you mind?"

"If you must."

An amused half-smile played on his lips—so attractive she felt a stab of disappointment when it disappeared.

"Miss Collins—"

"Chelsea," she corrected. "It would be silly to continue addressing me formally when you'll be seeing quite a bit of me."

He nodded, took another drag, and released it away from her face. He'd try reason first. "Chelsea,

I'm prepared to offer you more than your father's will stipulates—if you stay out of the business. The money will come through in two years. So, if you're concerned that you won't come out ahead financially unless you work here, let me relieve your mind.'' He flicked a few ashes into an amber glass ashtray. ''We'll have the papers drawn up tomorrow and you can be on your way back to Richmond by the end of the week.''

She'd been dismissed with as much thought as his cigarette ashes. Her heart sank when she realized the uphill battle she faced. He couldn't possibly know how important this was to her. ''I'm not going back to Richmond. I want to make a place for myself here in Arizona. My apartment in Richmond has been sublet and I quit my last modeling assignment. So, I need this job.''

''You need a job?'' He rubbed a large hand over his eyes. ''Would you tell me why a model would get involved in putting together buildings? That's what we do, you know. Not interior decorating. And,'' he added, stubbing out his cigarette, ''what makes you think *you've* got the background for this business?''

''Well, I can't seriously pursue a career in modeling,'' she said. Unhappy with being forced to expose her inadequacies to such an unsympathetic man, she stood and walked to a wall lined with books. ''You see, I'm flawed.''

She looked over her shoulder and watched his thick eyebrows furrow together as he inspected her closely once again. His intent gaze drifted over her fitted white dress and slim legs, then swept back up to her face. When his eyes lingered on her crimson mouth, her heart gave an odd little jump.

His dark eyes asked the unspoken question and she forced a laugh past her tight throat. "I'm not tall enough," she explained. "I'd need at least four more inches before I could make a real career of modeling." Briefly scanning the bookshelves, she noticed with surprise a book of philosophy squeezed in among the volumes on small business management and construction. She tucked that observation in the back of her mind.

Then, turning back to him, she finished her explanation of her flaws. "Something about proportion and long legs."

Jake tore his gaze from the most shapely pair of legs he'd ever seen back to her uncertain eyes. He felt an ominous tug in the region of his heart at the way Chelsea kept trying to hide how vulnerable she felt. She was trying so hard to be pleasant. And he knew he wasn't helping one bit. A twinge of guilt sneaked in, but he quickly banished it before it could take hold. As cruel as it seemed, he'd save them both a lot of trouble if he let her know she wasn't needed here.

He deliberately made his voice harsh. "And your background?"

"I don't suppose Lincoln Logs when I was nine counts," she said in an attempt at levity.

Jake didn't respond.

"As far as my background is concerned, I think both you and I know the only thing that qualifies me for working at Collins and Slater is my father's will. And of course, legally, the will is the bottom line."

He impatiently drummed a pencil on his desk.

She forged on, sounding more confident than she felt. "However, a reasonable person might surmise that I'm at least trainable since I completed my degree in fine arts. Anyway, it shouldn't take me but a few days to settle into the guest house and then I'll be ready to—"

"Guest house?" He gripped the pencil so tightly it snapped.

Staring at his hands, she responded slowly. "Well, yes. Since I inherited the guest house, it seemed only natural that I would live there."

"The guest house is on my property," he said tightly, kissing his privacy good-bye.

"Oh, is that a problem?"

He rubbed his face again. "Don't you think you'd be more comfortable in town? After all, the property is miles away, and nobody's been in the guest house for two months. There could be all kinds of critters in there." He paused meaningfully. "You know we have rattlers in Arizona. And we've probably got the largest population of black widow spiders in the fifty states."

Chelsea's stomach rolled at the thought of spiders and snakes. She reconsidered staying at the guest house until she caught the calculated expression on his face.

"It's sweet of you to be concerned, but I'm sure I'll manage."

When his face fell in disappointment, she silently congratulated herself on seeing through his intentions. Briskly, she said, "Now, if you'll just give me directions, I'll get out of your hair."

"Chelsea, I'll be blunt," he said in a last ditch effort, "I don't want you anywhere near my business or my home, but your father's tied my hands with that will of his."

For the smallest moment, she felt a measure of sympathy for him. The man was obviously frustrated. At least she hoped he didn't behave this way on a regular basis. He'd apparently had a busy day, coupled with her arrival and subsequent invasion into his life. His control was stretched to the limit, and she could tell that if he owned just one percent more of the business, he would cheerfully kick her out of his office.

She shrugged her shoulders and offered what reassurance she could. "You've made your opinion clear. I'll just have to do my best to change your mind. Now, about those directions?"

She turned at the sound of a knock on his door. A middle-aged, potbellied man with a cap on his head strolled into the room. "Jake, I finished fixing the truck, but the hardware supplier's messed up the order again. Juan's about ready to strip the skin off the delivery guy. You'd better get out there before he gets himself hauled off to jail."

Jake looked at the ceiling, then flicked his gaze over Chelsea again.

Her heart thumped erratically.

"We'll talk later," he said and left.

Trying to decide if her trembling was due to fear or anticipation, Chelsea stared after him. Then, feeling the older man's stare, she turned her attention to him. "Mr. uh, Al—"

"Walker," he finished for her and smiled broadly as he pushed his cap further back on his head. "If it isn't little Chelsea Collins all grown up."

At last, someone nice, she thought and returned his smile. "How did you know?"

He swelled with pride. "Well, I was one of Ed's best friends and he was always showing me pictures." His smile faded momentarily. "Of course, he hadn't shown me many in the last few years. But I'd know you even if I hadn't seen your picture. You've got your daddy's eyes."

His statement pleased her and she extended her hand. "It's a pleasure to meet you, Mr. Walker. And it means a lot to know my father had such a faithful friend."

After rubbing his greasy hand on the side of his pants, Al clutched hers and pumped furiously. When he released it, she dropped her hand to her side. Realizing too late her mistake, Chelsea glanced down at the black stain on her favorite white dress. She ignored it, not wanting to make the older man uncomfortable.

"Mr. Walker, if you would be so kind as to give me directions to Jake's property?"

"Sure thing."

Al drew a map for her, then Chelsea thanked him and bade him good-bye after they left Jake's office building through the connecting garage.

Al stood beside Jake as both men watched her

mesmerizing stride from the garage area. "She sure turned out pretty," Al said.

"Hmm," Jake said.

"What'd you say?"

"Nothing," Jake answered with a dark expression on his face. He noted the wolf whistles that rang through the air. And because he wasn't blind, he also noted that Chelsea Collins had curves in all the right places. She was the kind of woman who opened doors with just a smile. The kind that made every man around suck in his gut and stand a little taller.

She was going to be hell to deal with.

"Looks like she wants to get in the swing of things here."

"Not if I can help it," Jake muttered.

"What about the will?" Al asked. "Doesn't she own half of the business?"

"Fifty-one percent," Jake corrected flatly and scowled.

Al nudged his cap farther back on his head. "She's got her daddy's eyes, ya know?"

Jake's expression softened at the mention of his former partner and he relaxed his stance. As much as the prospect of Chelsea's invasion into his life annoyed him, he couldn't forget that she was Ed Collins's daughter. And Ed Collins had given him a hand when nobody else would. Now, if he could just figure out what to do with his daughter.

When Jake patted his pockets for his cigarettes, Al commented, "Hey, I thought you were trying to quit."

Jake gave a rare, wry grin as he remembered Chelsea's displeasure with his smoking. "Yeah, well, this habit may come in handy in the next few weeks."

* * *

Jake's land seemed desolate. Accustomed to the green grass and trees of Virginia, Chelsea shook her head at the rough terrain. Few trees and little grass. Rough like Jake. Big and powerful. Like the construction business and the desert, he was in many ways foreign to her. He was also blatantly male. Not her type, she sniffed, as she braked in front of the smaller of two buildings.

She smiled at the writer of the will's notion of a guest house. In this case, it was an attachment to the back of the garage. Clutching a suitcase, she headed for the door.

She stopped abruptly when a large wolf-like animal approached her. The animal barked loudly and Chelsea cringed in fear. "Oh, God," she whispered, closing her eyes. "I've traveled across the entire United States and burned my bridges in Richmond, so I can get eaten by a desert wolf."

The animal ceased its growling and came closer to sniff her. Chelsea stood stock still trying to decide what to do. Should she bang him with her suitcase? While she continued her internal debate, he let out a whimper and licked her hand. She opened her eyes and stared at the animal.

She gave a witless giggle of relief. This wasn't a desert wolf. He was a just a mixed-breed dog with an emphasis on German shepherd. She petted his head. "You scared me there for a minute. I was sure you were a wild animal." The dog seemed to bark in disagreement with her.

Laughing, she bent down. "You don't look a bit like my mother's little shih tzu, Fifi." He responded to her voice by jumping up and rubbing his paws against her.

"Oh, no," she moaned, when she saw the pawprints. "I guess this dress just bit the dust." She noticed the silver circle hanging from his collar and read it out loud: "Mozart."

He barked and Chelsea laughed at him. Who ever heard of naming a dog Mozart? "Tell me something, Mozart, is your owner all bark and no bite like you? I hope so." Chelsea petted him again and moved toward the garage.

After she opened the door, Chelsea took a deep breath and braced herself for the rush of emotion she expected to feel at being in her father's home.

When it didn't come, she relaxed slightly and walked into the house. A tiny kitchen and bar faced a den furnished simply with a beige sofa and chair, two end tables and a television. Farther down the hall, she found a small bedroom and bath with, thank God, a bathtub.

She saw nothing of her jovial father in this bare living space. No pictures, no clothes in the closet, nothing. A vague disappointment assailed her. She'd hoped to learn something of Ed Collins, the father she'd seen only two weeks out of every year until the last few years.

Her mother had vehemently protested Chelsea's decision to accept the challenge in her father's will and move to Arizona. Vivien's voice rang through her mind. "This is just a wild goose chase of yours, Chelsea. Why can't you settle down with one of these nice young men your father and I have introduced to you in the last year?"

Chelsea hadn't bothered arguing. Though she'd had to bite her tongue at her mother's inaccurate reference to her stepfather, she'd just let Vivien rattle on while Chelsea continued packing. Vivien had left in a huff.

And here Chelsea stood after a five-day drive across country with most of her prized possessions and clothing crammed into her small car. Like a gambler putting all her chips on one number, she'd put all her hopes on making a place for herself in White Bluff. With reluctance, she'd traded in her flashy sports car for a more practical model. But making major adjustments in her life wasn't new to her. She felt a tinge of sadness when she thought of the dancing career she'd been forced to abandon. Glancing down at her imperfect ankle, she smiled ruefully.

A wave of homesickness passed over her as she realized she had no friends in her desolate new home. Then she shrugged it off and went to change her clothes. She chastised herself for her melancholy mood. Her father may have neglected to leave his stamp on his living space, but Chelsea intended to make this a welcoming home for herself. She had a feeling she'd need a haven in the coming weeks.

After a thorough dusting and scrubbing, the guest house began to shine, and Chelsea enjoyed the lemony smell that permeated the air. She heard a car door slam and peeked through a window. Jake walked to the front door of his sprawling house.

He appeared tired, she thought. He bent his head, squeezed the back of his neck with a large hand, and stretched his muscular body. He had a certain appeal, she supposed. Even Chelsea had to appreciate those linebacker shoulders, well-developed pecs, and slim hips.

She'd observed enough of him to know he was a no-nonsense kind of man with no patience for frivolities. Her father had told her that Jake didn't manage Collins and Slater from afar, but threw himself right into the middle of it.

Even with his rough exterior, she sensed something solid and reassuring about him. It would be nice if they could be friends, but she knew that was just wishful thinking. Jake viewed her as one of those frivolities with which he had no patience.

Still, something about his eyes challenged Chelsea and she wanted to prove he was wrong about her.

By the afternoon of her third day in White Bluff, Chelsea was so tired of her own company she was ready to start talking to the woodwork. She fixed herself a southern meal to lift her spirits and was just removing the biscuits from the oven when she heard a knock at the door.

She brushed back a strand escaping from her ponytail and answered the door. Jake stood outside—hair damp, shirt sleeves rolled up his forearms, and the jeans he wore did nothing to hide his masculinity.

Her mouth went a little dry, but she managed to get the proper words out. "Jake, come in. What can I do for you?"

He entered, filling her kitchen with his presence. By his size alone, he was the kind of man who made a woman acutely aware of her femininity. She looked at him expectantly.

He rested his hands on his lean hips and looked around. "You've done a lot already. Al's wife, Janelle, went through all Ed's clothes and packed up his personal things right after he died." He looked at Chelsea. "I've got some boxes of his pictures and mementos in the house if you want to go through them sometime."

"Thank you. I'd appreciate that."

He sighed and turned away as if he felt uncomfortable. "Uh, I was kind of rough on you the other day, with you being so far away from home." His voice was rough but sincere. "It was a busy day. The truck and front-loader broke down and my best mechanic took an unexpected trip to Tijuana. I wasn't at my best."

Chelsea smiled slightly. This was as close as Jake was going to come to an apology. "I could tell by the comments you made from under the car that the day wasn't going as planned." When he turned around to face her, she could have sworn his high cheekbones were ruddier. "I also got the impression that my arrival didn't improve matters."

He cleared his throat and searched for something else to say. Then he sniffed appreciatively, finally noticing the hot biscuits she'd just removed from the oven. "What are you cooking?"

Her smile broadened at his interest in her food and she decided to give him a peace offering. "Fried chicken, mashed potatoes and gravy, green beans, and biscuits."

His eyes practically devoured the food as she spoke. "You fixed all that and you're eating by yourself?"

She strolled over to the stove, lifted the top off the chicken, and allowed the tempting aroma to waft through the air. "I have enough for company, but I haven't made any friends yet." She smiled at him engagingly. "Can you think of anyone who wouldn't mind sharing it with me?"

Only about half a dozen anyones, Jake thought as his gaze fell over her. A man would kill for that smile, let alone her body. She'd shed her sophisticated image from the first day they'd met. Now, with her blonde hair pulled back into a ponytail, her makeup-free face, and shorts and tank top, her femininity had a wholesome edge. But not too wholesome, Jake thought, as he took in the thrust of her breasts and her shapely legs.

He felt a surge of discomfort at his unwelcome attraction to her. It would probably be best if he turned down her invitation to dinner. Another whiff of fried chicken teased his nostrils and Jake almost groaned. There was no way he could face another can of beans tonight when this was the alternative.

"I could help you out."

"Well, I wouldn't want you to put yourself out, Jake," she drawled.

A smile quirked along the edges of his mouth. "Quit teasing me, Chelsea. You know I'm practically foaming at the mouth." And not just over the food, he thought.

Her laugh tingled pleasantly through the air. "Go ahead and sit down at the bar. Everything's ready except the drinks." She turned to the refrigerator. "Iced tea, juice, or milk?"

"No beer?"

"No, I've got some wine."

"I'll take that." He patted his pockets and looked around for an ashtray. "Where's your ashtray?"

Chelsea turned around with the bottle of wine. "No ashtrays."

Jake figured if she were the type to give lectures, she'd be giving one right now. But she held her tongue, so he shrugged his shoulders. "I'm working on quitting anyway."

"That's commendable." When she saw his raised eyebrow, she decided to change the subject. "Tell me what happened at work today."

So Chelsea proceeded with prodding questions resulting in one- or two-word replies from Jake, gaining a minimal understanding of a day in the life of a general contractor. When they neared the end of the meal, she wondered if he was always so stingy with his conversation. And she felt genuine bewilderment when she noticed just how much of her food he had consumed.

Melancholy edged in as she realized when Jake

finished eating she'd be left alone again. Chelsea tried another question. "Do you have any family nearby?"

"No."

She rolled her eyes in frustration as she removed the plates from the bar. One of her finishing-school instructors had sworn Chelsea could charm a response from a wall. Chelsea was seriously beginning to doubt her ability, so she dealt with her failure graciously, giving Jake an opportunity to leave. "Well, Jake, I've enjoyed having you for dinner. I hope you'll be able to come again sometime."

Jake shifted uncomfortably at the forlorn expression on her pretty face. He'd never been much for dinner conversation. While her perfume made him think of wildflowers and moonlit nights, her sultry voice conjured up visions of satin sheets and lazy loving. Even though Chelsea had tried to put him at ease throughout the meal, he'd been so aware of her femininity every time she spoke that he'd felt it necessary to create space between them.

He'd obviously accomplished that in spades. Jake, however, had always had a weakness for strays. It probably had something to do with his upbringing. Lord knows, he'd always felt like a stray. In spite of her polish and beauty, Chelsea looked like an abandoned kitten.

He cursed his susceptibility to her, then sighed in surrender. Maybe if he invited her to a softball game she'd meet some other people and he wouldn't feel quite so responsible for her loneliness. "Uh, I'm getting ready to go to a softball game. We've had a company sponsored team for a few years now.''

There was a long silence. ''You wouldn't want to go, would you?''

She'd never received a less enthusiastic invitation in her life. But she was so thrilled at the prospect of getting out among people, she would have accepted an invitation to a mud-wrestling match. ''I'd love to go. Do I need to change?''

His gaze fell over her slowly, lingering on her bare feet long enough to make her toes curl. ''You just need some sneakers.''

Chelsea nodded and quickly filled the sink with water.

''Hey, we've got at least a half hour before we need to leave. You don't have to be in such a rush. I'll go home and change shirts.''

Jake rose from the table. ''I wouldn't have thought you could cook.''

That made her pause and she turned back to look at him, her brows furrowed. ''Why wouldn't I know how to cook?''

He shrugged his impressive shoulders. ''I just didn't get the impression that you . . .''

''That I could do anything useful,'' Chelsea finished for him. When he didn't deny it, she had to check her anger. ''You know, Jake, I wouldn't have thought a six-and-a-half foot general contractor would be the type of man to read books on philosophy, let alone own them.'' She smiled guilelessly. ''We might just surprise each other yet.''

An almost-grin tugged at the corners of his mouth, making her yearn to see a genuine smile. "Thirty minutes, Chelsea." He turned to leave. "And I'm six three."

TWO

Chelsea leaned back against the wooden bleachers and pulled her visor firmly in place. Curious gazes had followed her arrival with Jake. Although he'd left her as soon as they arrived, she'd met almost everyone at the field. Al Walker's daughter, Anita, walked over after the fourth inning, and welcomed Chelsea to White Bluff. The two women made arrangements to meet for lunch and Chelsea began to believe she just might be able to make this new life work out.

Jake played hard, hitting two home runs. What was the saying? Play hard, work hard, love hard. What kind of lover would he be? The question teased her outrageously as the game ended with Jake's team winning over the mayor's office team. Chelsea mentally scoffed at herself, but couldn't prevent a little shiver at Jake's take-me-as-I-am sexual appeal.

A smooth male voice interrupted her thoughts. "Heaven has arrived in White Bluff. Tell me, lovely lady, what did we do to deserve you?"

He was blond, tanned, and trim. Chelsea smiled in response. He was also a total flirt. This was the kind of man she'd dated in Richmond. Very smooth, sophisticated, unthreatening to Chelsea. "I'm not sure everyone would agree with your concept of heaven, but I'm here because I've just been made a partner of Collins and Slater Contractors."

"You're kidding?" he said and offered his hand to her as she jumped from the bleachers.

"No joke, I'm Chelsea Collins."

"So, you're Ed's daughter." He studied her closely. "You know, you've got his—"

"Eyes," she finished with a sad smile.

"I guess you've heard it before. I'm sorry about your father's death. He was well-liked in the community. He served on several committees for community improvement."

"Thank you. And you're?"

He touched his forehead and smiled ruefully. "You've addled my brain with your beauty. Chris Preston, public defender, at your service." He took her hand and lightly kissed her knuckles.

She chuckled, but felt not even one tingle. Retrieving her hand, she looked around for Jake. "It's a pleasure to meet you Chris, but I'm looking for my ride right now. Have you seen Jake Slater?"

"He's your ride?" Chris asked in disbelief.

"Yes," she answered slowly. "Is there any reason he shouldn't be?"

Chris covered his mouth and cleared his throat. "Well, no, but—"

"Oh, there he is." Chelsea spotted Jake coming in her direction and smiled at Chris before she turned to leave. "It was nice meeting you, Chris. I'm sure I'll be seeing you around."

"Count on it," he called after her.

After pats on the back and some good-natured jesting, Jake and Chelsea started home. "That was a good game. Do you beat everyone that easily?" Chelsea looked at Jake as he slowed down for a stop light. She wondered when she'd ridden in a jeep before and realized, with a little grin, that she never had. Her dates, usually foisted on her by her mother and stepfather, had driven expensive sports cars or luxury sedans.

"Not everyone," he answered and shifted the gear. He looked at her with a glint of curiosity in his dark eyes. "I wouldn't have thought you'd be familiar with softball or baseball."

His assessing gaze made her feel incredibly feminine. "Oh sure," she said, tongue in cheek. "I've never touched a baseball. I only had tea parties and played with dolls. And I never got dirty. Swing a bat, heaven forbid."

His lips twitched, then stretched into a grin. "I think the lady's pulling my leg."

"Wouldn't that be too much exercise for me?"

"What?"

"Pulling your leg." Chelsea glanced down at his powerful thighs and felt a tingle in spite of herself.

"I don't know, Jake. You've got very long legs. That might constitute manual labor."

Jake chuckled. "Okay, you've proved your point. So where'd you learn about baseball?"

Teasing that laugh out of him gave her a rush. "My father felt it was his responsibility to educate me on the finer points of life when he visited me in Richmond. Since he often visited in the summer, we usually took in a baseball game." Chelsea smiled in reminiscence. "A couple of summers, he even tried to teach me how to play softball."

"Did you like it?" The light changed and Jake accelerated.

"Hmm?"

"Did you like it? Going to baseball games, learning how to play softball?"

Chelsea sighed. "Oh, I loved going anywhere with my dad. He fussed a lot, but he was proud when I finally learned how to choke up on the bat and hit." She paused for a moment. "I think he would have liked a son."

Jake heard the wistful tone in her voice and fought the urge to reassure and sympathize. With her gentle sense of humor and sunny disposition, she could easily lead him astray. Still, Jake was confident she'd ruin his business with her ignorance, given half a chance. He wouldn't be rude to her, but he'd discourage her presence in Arizona and in his company at every turn. She didn't belong here.

"You never came to see him," he finally said.

Chelsea closed her eyes and took a deep breath at

the sharp pain. "No," she replied in a low voice and turned her misery-filled eyes to the window.

The next afternoon Chelsea dressed more appropriately, in lightweight slacks and a colorful cotton blouse. She glanced wistfully at her heels and put on tennis shoes instead. In the midst of the male-dominated construction world, she could have used every inch she could possibly add to her height.

Because of the heat, the construction workers finished their workday by early afternoon. Jake's work, however, didn't stop then. He had bids to check on, deliveries to receive, and telephone calls to return.

Chelsea made her way through the small office building to the connecting warehouse and garage and gave a start. She was going to have to get used to the construction worker's attire. Several young men busily hauled material from one truck to another wearing bandanas around their heads, low-slung shorts, and workboots. And nothing else.

Unobtrusively, she walked around the work area until she spotted Al muttering to himself as he perched on a forklift. When he looked up and saw Chelsea, his face cleared.

"Chelsea!" Al exclaimed. "I didn't know you were back here." He smiled broadly and tipped his cap back. "Whatcha doing?"

She couldn't help but smile in return. "I'm ready to go to work. But Jake's too busy to give me anything to do yet." Chelsea sensed the opportunity for a friendship with this paunchy, frank older man.

"Al, it's very important to me to be successful here. Can I count on you to help me out?"

Al puffed his chest out and wore a serious, prideful expression. "Your daddy was my best friend, and there isn't much I wouldn't do to help out his little girl."

Chelsea arched her eyebrow at his description of her and he coughed self-consciously. "Uh, his daughter," he corrected. "With Jake working twelve-hour days, there's bound to be something you can do here. He'll probably talk with you as soon as he finishes with that delivery guy."

Chelsea shrugged. "Jake hasn't mentioned what he has planned for me. He just told me to show up here this afternoon," she smiled ruefully, "and not to wear any more short skirts."

Al's lips twitched. "Well, he's got a point there. The boys teased Jake about keeping you to himself the other day. He looked like a storm cloud ready to burst by the end of the day."

Al turned away and yelled, "Bill, put that equipment on the other truck. It's going to the Dancy site tomorrow."

Chelsea watched the younger man obediently change direction. "How do they know where to put everything?"

"That's easy," Al replied. "We just tell them."

They shared a smile and Chelsea stood by his side for the next few minutes while Al directed traffic. There was an air of purpose and cooperation throughout the entire process and she found herself wanting to be a part of it. When one of the men yelled something about damaged merchandise, Al strode over to inspect it.

She backed out of the way of another oncoming forklift when suddenly she heard a loud crack. Automatically, she looked up and saw the heavily burdened lift falling toward her.

For a fraction of a second, Chelsea froze. She felt something like steel wrap around her stomach, knocking the air out of her and swinging her away from the descending lift.

She gasped for air as she hung limp as a ragdoll, her feet dangling inches from the floor. When the oxygen connected with her brain, she noted the oaths uttered from Jake's mouth as he stared at the tilted forklift.

She flapped her arms a little to get his attention, but he just kept holding her so tight she could barely breathe. The rest of the workers crowded around and Chelsea began to wonder if she'd become invisible. They were all so concerned about the blasted lift that they didn't notice her flopping around like a fish out of water.

Acutely conscious of his strong hand clamped just under her breasts, she rasped out his name, ''Jake!'' Chelsea pinched a rock hard thigh when he didn't respond. ''Jake!''

He finally looked at her, and a strange current passed between them and tangled. His eyes searched hers. The heat of his gaze seared her. She watched his gaze drop to where his hand was clasped under her breast and her heart beat double time.

The sound of someone clearing his throat broke

the intensity of the moment. Jake set her down gently and ran his hands over her shoulders and arms, sending off tiny sparks with each touch. His dark eyes were full of concern. "Are you okay? I might have been kinda rough, but that was going straight for your head."

Chelsea looked up at the lift and felt sick when she saw that, though it hadn't fallen to the floor, it had shifted enough that she could have been seriously injured. She wrapped her arms protectively around herself and looked back at Jake.

"Uh, thank you for moving me out of the way." She clenched her hands to keep them from shaking. "Do you mind if I go to your office?"

"Sure, I'll go with you." He turned to the work crew. "Hey, you guys stay away from here until we can get this fixed. I don't need any more close calls today." They mumbled their agreement. Jake took her elbow in his strong hand and guided her to his office. His touch sent another tingle down her arm and Chelsea struggled with the surprising sensation.

She felt so soft, Jake thought. And she weighed so little, he'd forgotten he was holding her after he'd pulled her away from that tilting load. Every muscle in his body clenched at the image of that lift crashing down on her pretty blonde head.

She didn't belong here. He wasn't sure why she'd come or what had possessed Ed Collins to bequeath fifty-one percent of the business to her and to even suggest she get involved in contracting. Jake shook his head. Although he disagreed with his former partner's decisions, the least he could do was keep Chelsea Collins from killing herself.

Jake opened his office door and stepped aside. He was banking on Chelsea tiring of everything about White Bluff, Arizona. He figured she was amusing herself until something better came along. He just hoped it would come soon.

She stumbled a little as she entered his office. His hands naturally reached out to steady her. Instinct made him draw her against his chest when he saw how shaken she was.

Chelsea leaned against him for just a moment, drawing reassurance from the solid male length of his body. "I'm sorry," she murmured and moved away.

"No. It's okay," he said from a tight throat and reluctantly removed his hands. He'd felt satisfyingly protective with her in his arms. The memory of her breasts crushed against him wouldn't easily fade, he predicted. Giving his hands something to do, Jake poured her a cup of coffee.

Chelsea slumped into a chair. She took the cup, and after blowing on the contents, carefully sipped.

"Thanks again," she murmured. In an attempt to lighten the strained atmosphere, she teased, "I never knew how exciting things could get during a delivery."

Jake poured his own cup, then leaned against his desk. "That was a little close for comfort, Chelsea. Don't you think you'd be better off in Richmond?"

Her blue eyes flashed astonishment. "Are you kidding? I just got here." She took in his unconvinced expression and tossed her head. "I'm not letting a near-accident send me running, if that's what you had in mind." Uncomfortable with how his body loomed over her, she set her cup down and stood. "I'm here for the duration, Jake. A year, hopefully longer." The uneasiness flickered in his eyes again and Chelsea tamped down her frustration.

Sighing, he turned away, patting his pockets in search of his cigarettes. He scowled when he realized they weren't there, and dragged several thick volumes from his shelves. He pivoted back around to face her and stared into her eyes. "Read these. When you finish you can do inventory."

"Inventory?" she repeated.

"Inventory." Jake's eyes grew hard as he emphasized his next words. "You report to me, and I don't want to see you inside the garage again."

Chelsea had never been a violent person, but she found herself longing for her spiked heels, toying with the notion of grinding them into his feet.

Taking a deep breath, she reluctantly faced facts. While Jake knew everything about contracting, she knew nothing. She was forced to let him call the shots, but she felt she deserved a little courtesy.

"Inventory," Chelsea said again and swallowed it with difficulty. "You know, Jake, since we're partners, we'll be getting to know each other pretty well. I'll have to get used to your . . . personality." She used the term personality loosely. "And since I'm the majority owner," she said and watched him cringe, "you'll have to adjust to a few of my eccentricities.

"Where I come from, when we ask someone to

do something, we use a word. I'm sure you've heard it before," she drawled. "Please."

He gritted his teeth and stared mutinously.

Chelsea crossed her arms over her chest and waited as if she had all the time in the world.

After a long silence, the word was torn from him. "Please."

She beamed.

He glowered.

Two weeks later, Jake joined Al at Rosie's Bar for a beer after work. When Jake lit a cigarette, Al raised his eyebrows. "I thought you were giving up smoking. Seems like you've turned into a regular chimney the last week or so."

Jake gave Al a withering glance. Al knew why Jake was smoking so much lately. Something about a little blonde all set to turn his business inside out. "We've discussed this before. As soon as my partner gives up her little charade, I'll quit."

Al took a long drink from his foaming mug and set it down on the scarred wooden table. "Don't you think you're being kinda hard on the girl? She hasn't been too much trouble since you gave her something to do."

"I figured she wouldn't last a day doing such a mundane job." Jake shook his head. "She's more stubborn than I thought."

"Stubborn or determined," Al corrected. "Janelle and I had her over for dinner the other night. She looks like a featherbrain, but she ain't. She's digging her heels in deep in White Bluff. I hear she's even working with some kids down at the community center already.''

Jake had wondered where she'd gone on the few nights she'd left the guest house. Though he tried to pretend she didn't live practically on his doorstep, he found himself watching for her return.

Chelsea Collins was turning out to be more complicated than he'd planned. So far, she'd been prompt for work every day, performing her task of counting inventory without complaint. His only complaint was that most of his men were falling over themselves trying to find excuses to be near her. But what really irritated him was that he could understand why they wanted to be near her. She was beautiful, and there weren't that many beautiful women in White Bluff, Arizona.

Her low southern drawl ran down a man's nerve endings like honey. And she was friendly. Jake grimaced. Friendly enough that every unattached man who worked for him, along with some of the married ones, had asked her out. He wasn't sure how she'd done it, but she'd managed to turn down every single offer without offending anyone.

The only two hold-outs to her charm were Jerry Mendez, a young boy on probation Jake had hired, and himself. And damned if he wasn't charmed himself. The way she moved that curvy body of hers should be illegal. Although her beauty and actions didn't seem calculated, he suspected they were all part of a grand design for her to get what she wanted—all of his business.

Al interrupted his thoughts. ''What do you think

she's gonna do when she finds out your inventory's computerized and she's been counting staples for nothing?''

Jake couldn't conceal his grin. "I imagine she'll be angry. She might even be angry enough to go back to Richmond.''

Al looked at him with disgust. "I can't believe you're doing this to Ed Collins's daughter after all he did for you.''

At the mention of his late friend, Jake's rare grin fell. Al was right. Not only had Ed Collins given him a job when no one else would, he'd been a mentor and a father figure. When Jake's mother had finally died after a long battle with cancer, there had been nowhere for him to turn. At age sixteen, he was too old to want to get involved in foster care and too young and inexperienced to earn a decent wage. Ed had kept tabs on Jake after the boy's mother died. When he'd noticed Jake hanging around with a rough group of teenagers, he offered Jake a job and a place to stay.

Jake sighed. "I know all about what Ed did for me. He helped me get a college scholarship so I could get my business degree at night. He let me invest in his business so we could expand. Hell, I don't know what would have happened to me if Ed Collins hadn't taken me in like a son.''

His thoughts drifted to the source of his current problem. Jake had been well acquainted with Chelsea Collins long before she arrived in White Bluff. Ed had enthusiastically shared his daughter's achievements and pictures with Jake—to the point where the younger man had felt envious. But if Chelsea was so wonderful, why hadn't she been bothered to pay her old man a visit once in a while? Not once had the blue-eyed, blonde-haired wonder shown up when Ed was alive. Hell, she hadn't even made it to the funeral.

Jake's envy had dissipated when he realized he was the lucky one, not Chelsea. She'd only had her father for an annual two-week visit in Richmond, while Jake had access to Ed's sense of humor and shrewd business instincts every day.

Shrugging off the guilt, he defended his actions. "Ed would expect her to pull her load. He'd test her mettle and dedication. That's all I'm doing. If she's got what it takes, she'll stay." He tipped his head back to finish his beer. "I'm just not going to let her mess up anything while she's trying out her wings."

The next afternoon, Chelsea counted ceiling tiles, lamely reminding herself that this kind of thing probably built character. She might have to be committed to a mental institution, but she'd be an insane person with character. Enormous character, she thought. Electric wire was next.

She caught sight of Al as he tipped his hat to her and held the door for a departing salesman. Chelsea cast him a wan, welcoming smile. Then she heard the salesman call out as he left the warehouse, "Hey, Jake, why do you have Chelsea counting ceiling tiles? I thought you had a computerized inventory."

The door swung shut and Chelsea froze. She looked down at the hundreds of ceiling tiles she'd counted. With an expression of pure disbelief, she turned her gaze to Al. When he shifted his feet and looked away, a fist of anger hit her so hard she saw red.

"Tell me I didn't hear that, Al."

Al studied her warily, then nodded.

Incensed, her voice rose in pitch and volume. "You mean I've spent the last two weeks counting carpentry supplies and staples for nothing?"

Al nodded again.

"You're telling me my father's partner is so afraid I'll destroy his business, he's giving me a job that doesn't even exist?" Chelsea's voice sounded shrill to her own ears. She was so angry and frustrated she had to blink back her tears.

Al saw the emotion brimming from her and gave her an awkward hug. "Now, now," he comforted. "Jake doesn't mean to be malicious. You've knocked him for a loop and he just hasn't figured out what to do with you."

Hearing Al defend Jake only increased her anger and she pulled away from the older man. "Well, he could at least be honest with me." Chelsea's eyes could have burned a hole through the door leading to the office. "He may be the managing partner, but I don't have to stand for this." She pushed up her sleeves and turned to leave.

"That's exactly what he's expecting."

Chelsea whirled back around. "What do you mean?"

"He's expecting you to either get tired of this menial job or furious when you find out you've been doing inventory for nothing. He figures this is some whim and you'll go back to Richmond before the month is out.''

Struggling to keep a lid on her escalating anger, Chelsea closed her eyes and took a deep breath. The anger was one thing, but the feeling of betrayal cut like a knife. She opened her eyes and looked directly at Al. "It's very important to me to make a place for myself here. After all, I do own over half of the business. Is there any possibility that Jake is ever going to let me have a meaningful position in this company?"

Al sighed. "I don't know. The only way you'll make it here is if you can prove there's more to you than what meets the eye.'' He winked and smiled. "Although what meets the eye ain't bad.'' He cocked his head to one side. "I don't blame you for wanting a little revenge. He deserves it. But you can't go off half-cocked. You need to plan it out. Use that brain of yours and remember that under Jake's tough exterior, he's got a good heart. Okay?''

Good heart, my fanny. Still, Al was right about going off half-cocked. She needed a plan. Chelsea nodded absently as he left.

She avoided Jake like the plague, leaving her reports on his desk when he wasn't there. She made sure she was busy every evening. Needing an outlet for her excess energy, she went to the community center and danced for hours every night. She'd welcomed the opportunity to provide ballet lessons for children who couldn't afford them, fully realizing she would have to be careful or her ankle would go out on her.

After a lengthy session one evening, she limped into the guest house, wincing at the pain and berating herself for pushing too hard. Propping the weak ankle on the sofa, she applied an ice pack and relaxed.

When she heard a knock at her door, she dragged herself off the couch and answered it, too tired to be concerned about her skimpy leotard and tights. It was Jake. And she was surprised at the force of the pleasure she felt just seeing him again. Despite his deception, she felt the tug from his dark eyes as surely as her own eyes were blue.

He rested his hands on his lean hips and slowly took in her appearance, from her tousled hair to her black leotard and pink tights. "I haven't seen you in a few days and I just wanted to make sure everything's okay."

"Everything's okay," she lied.

A flicker of disbelief passed through his eyes, but he didn't press. He pointed at the ice cap she held in her hand. "What's that for?"

"Oh, an old ankle injury. I just overworked it. Thanks for coming by. Now, if you'll excuse me—" Her polite little dismissal was cut off when Jake walked through the door and gently nudged her aside. He towered over her and she was struck once again by his intimidating size.

He looked down at the ankle she favored. "Let me see. It might be serious."

"It's not," she assured him quickly, wincing as

she tried to conceal her limp. Carefully making her way to the sofa, she gestured to a chair. "Have a seat."

"Not until I see that ankle."

His voice was firm. It irritated her that he was so concerned about her ankle, yet so insensitive to her needs at the office. "Jake, I've been taking care of this ankle since I was sixteen. An ice pack, an ace bandage, and some TLC for a couple of days, and it'll be fine."

He paused then sat down. "Did you hurt it dancing?"

"Initially or now?"

"Initially?"

"No, I broke it when Daddy took me hiking during my sixteenth summer." She smiled in remembrance. "I thought by the way he carried on that it hurt him more than it did me. Until I tried to dance on it, anyway."

"Were you good?"

"Yes," she said truthfully. "I'd been accepted by a prestigious ballet school in New York." She shrugged. "The ankle healed, but not well enough for performance ballet."

"You must have been disappointed." Jake touched her ankle with surprisingly gentle hands.

She stared at his large hand on her ankle. It felt incredibly warm. For one wild moment, she wished she could feel his calloused palm against her bare skin. Appalled, Chelsea jerked her attention back to the conversation.

"I was mostly frustrated because I couldn't make

my body do what it could before. And pushing myself only made it worse." She grimaced. "Sometimes, if I'm frustrated about something, I'll push again. But it reminds me every time."

"You should take better care of yourself."

Impatient with his orders, Chelsea was about to ignore her upbringing and tell him to mind his business, when the phone rang. Since he was sitting closest to it, he picked it up and answered. She watched his face harden and wondered who it could be.

"Yeah, she's right here," Jake said and held out the receiver for her. "It's Chris Preston. I'll see you tomorrow morning."

Watching his swift stride away from her, Chelsea couldn't help but be distracted by the controlled energy he emanated. Out of nowhere came an enormous urge to shake that control. She shook her head at the thought. Chris had asked her a question and was waiting for an answer. "Oh, I'm sorry, what did you say?"

Chelsea's husky chuckle rippled along Jake's skin and he allowed her screen door to swing closed as he left the guest house. He willed his tight muscles to relax and rolled his shoulders. Why should he care if the local district attorney was calling her? What was it to him if Chris had the ability to draw that delicious laugh from her inviting lips?

Jake whistled sharply for Mozart and stomped into his house to his weight room. He'd furnished his house in a thoroughly masculine yet inviting decor. Warm browns, gold pillows, and cream curtains. But the room where he made his escape when the pressures grew intense held an impressive assortment of barbells, a bench, and an exercise machine. He selected his weights, reclined on the bench, and began his repetitions, affirming to himself that Chelsea Collins didn't belong here, that she was a piece of cotton candy fluff, that she would be leaving soon.

That she had breasts that begged for a man's hands and mouth.

Jake pressed the bar up, then eased it back down. White Bluff wouldn't provide enough excitement for her. *Bet he could give her some excitement*, a wicked voice inside him taunted. Her curvy little bottom made his palms sweat.

Jake shook his head, then pressed and lowered. She'd never fit in at the construction shop.

Bet she'd fit perfectly in his arms, the voice interjected. Her shapely legs brought erotic pictures of her naked body entwined with his.

And so it went. By the time sweat was dripping from his body and his muscles were trembling from exertion, he still hadn't erased the image of her dressed in the clinging leotard. And his pectorals weren't the only part of him as hard as a rock.

Two afternoons later found Jake edgy and irritated. Though Chelsea worked steadily on the inventory, she'd resumed her tendency to stay away from him. She was never rude; she just somehow found a way to be wherever he wasn't.

He heard her soft southern drawl issue a welcome to one of his employees. Jake gritted his teeth.

There was no good reason for him to be so irritated

with her behavior. After all, by tucking her away to do the inventory, hadn't he hoped to keep her out of his hair? Now, he found himself missing the little conversations they'd shared at the end of the work day when she reported her progress. With her silky hair, warm blue eyes, and ready smile, she seemed to sprinkle a little sunshine on everyone she spoke to. Only she wasn't speaking to him.

Jake sighed with disgust at his ambivalence and brushed his thoughts aside. He had a business to run.

Gathering her reports, Chelsea made a face at the bags of plaster she'd been counting and walked toward Jake's office. The time had arrived, she thought with glee. She'd finally devised the perfect retribution for Jake Slater and she was ready to put her plan into action. She tucked in her shirt, shook back her hair, and knocked on his door.

"Who is it?" he barked.

"Chelsea," she called back cheerfully, refusing to be intimidated by his unwelcoming tone.

A long silence passed and she began to wonder if he'd heard when the door wooshed open and he said, "Come in." He gestured her toward a chair. "Would you like some coffee?"

She blinked. He actually appeared glad for her presence. Well, perhaps glad was stretching it, but he wasn't frowning. It seemed to Chelsea that his face had been set in a perpetual scowl since she'd arrived in White Bluff. Now his features wore an almost pleasant expression. She was amazed at how much more handsome he looked without that dark grimace. Why, a woman could get lost in those dark, seductive eyes of his. She was brought up short when he repeated his offer of coffee.

"Hmm, uh, no," she murmured and gave him an inviting smile as she remembered her purpose. "As a matter-of-fact, I was wondering if you'd like to come over for dinner tonight."

_____ THREE _____

She'd set the stage carefully with hot food, a robust burgundy wine, and a small arrangement of spring flowers she'd purchased from the florist on the way home. Her attire had even been planned to suit the part she'd play: a white cotton sundress with embroidered yellow roses. Thin spaghetti straps supported the modest bodice, while revealing the creamy skin of her back and shoulders.

The only thing she hadn't counted on was the tingling sensation on her skin that resulted from the appreciative glances he kept sending her way. She took a deep breath to clear her head. Jake was finishing his second portion of beef stroganoff.

The time had arrived for phase two of her plan.

Chelsea filled Jake's wine glass. "You know, Jake, the real reason I invited you here tonight was to thank you."

Jake regarded her with a blank expression. "For what?"

She felt a distinct flutter in her midsection every time he looked at her. Standing, she took her plate to the sink. "Well, even though you weren't very pleased about it, you've been very accepting of my desire to be involved in the business."

Not daring to glance at him, she continued as she sliced the pie she'd baked the night before. "You've been so fair with me. I mean, I imagine there are plenty of men who would feel threatened because I'm the majority owner. Though I can't imagine why," she added meaningfully, "since I've no desire to do anything to put the business at risk."

Chelsea bit back a smile as she heard the soft clatter of Jake's silverware on his plate. If he'd stopped eating, then she surely had his attention. "Some men would try to thwart a woman who wanted to take an active role in the business." She flashed him an admiring smile. "But not you. You've been completely honest and aboveboard. I understand now why Daddy thought so highly of you."

Jake cleared his throat.

Stepping closer, she wished she didn't find him so appealing with his freshly showered male scent, damp hair, and powerful body. She shrugged off the errant thoughts easily when she remembered the hundreds of heavy equipment replacement parts she'd counted just today. Chelsea placed the apple pie in front of him and took her final shot. "I'm sure he would be grateful to know you're treating his daughter this way.''

Reining in her feeling of triumph at the sight of Jake shifting uncomfortably, she asked brightly, ''Would you like some ice cream with that apple pie?''

''No, thanks.'' Jake picked up his fork, then he paused. ''Chelsea, I've been thinking, now that you've worked on the inventory for so long, maybe it's time for you to move on to something else.''

Oh no, she wasn't letting him off the hook that easily. ''But I haven't finished,'' Chelsea protested, ''and I wouldn't want to leave such an important job incomplete.''

Jake sighed and rubbed his chin. ''I could get someone else to finish later this year.''

''But don't you need to do the entire store at one time for the inventory to be effective?'' Chelsea smiled innocently. ''Is there something wrong with your pie?''

Jake looked down at his plate. ''Uh, no. I guess I'm not hungry anymore.''

''Then let me wrap it up for you.'' Reaching into the deep pocket of her dress, she pulled out the antacid and placed it on the table in front of Jake.

When he glanced at her with suspicion, she picked up his plate and moved away. But before she completed one step, she felt his hand clamp down around her wrist as he firmly tugged her into his lap. She almost dropped the pie, but he caught it and set it on the bar where they had eaten.

''How long have you known?''

Her heart thumped wildly. "Known what?" she asked and turned her head to study a dent in one of the cabinets.

He tangled her hair in his big hands and forced her to look at him. "About the inventory."

She felt some trepidation at being in such a vulnerable position with this mountain of a man, but she brushed it aside in anger. The heat flared in her cheeks and her eyes flashed blue fire. "Since the day I counted two thousand ceiling tiles."

Jake released her hair and shook his head. "Lord, that was five days ago. Why haven't you said anything before now?"

Chelsea tried to wiggle away, but he caught her at her waist. "Because I was so angry I thought I might say something rash. Al told me you hoped I'd get bored or mad enough to go back to Richmond."

She squirmed futilely. "Will you please let me up?"

Jake felt as if he'd been kicked in the gut by the wounded expression on her face and he hated himself for hurting her. Gently, he said, "It hurt your feelings, didn't it?"

She gave a small gasp. "No, I was angry."

"Hurt," Jake corrected and squeezed her waist.

"Angry," she retorted, thrusting up her chin.

Her fierce expression coupled with her vulnerable pink lips and fiery eyes provided a temptation he couldn't resist, and Jake's thick skin was pierced. "Well, let me see if I can do something about it."

When he touched his mouth to hers, Chelsea tried to twist away, but he held her firmly. His voice had an unusual huskiness to it as he spoke his next words against her mouth. "Let me kiss you, Chelsea."

He didn't ask, he coaxed, and Chelsea found his simple command more effective than anything else he could have done. And she felt herself turn to liquid in his arms; her mouth grew pliant as he took her lips.

His hands captured her nape and she shivered at his touch. He ran his seeking tongue along her lips coaxing her response, making her want more until she welcomed his gentle exploration. Needing to be closer, she twined her arms around his neck. The kiss went on and on until they finally came up for air.

They both drew deep breaths; their hearts hammering wildly, their skin flushed and heated. His hooded eyes trapped her and he bent his head toward her. "Just one more."

He teased and tasted her, sending her into a delicious spin where her only reality was Jake. She was surrounded by him. Her bottom was wedged into his strong thighs. His arms circled her body and his mouth delved deeply.

Her nipples hardened against the thin dress as the fire spread throughout her body. She instinctively pressed her swollen breasts into his hard chest and darted her tongue into his mouth.

He groaned approvingly at her active response and gentled the kiss until he could pull away.

Struggling to get a grip on her equilibrium, she held tightly to his shoulders. She watched Jake tilt back his head and take a deep breath. "Lord, Chelsea, where'd you learn to kiss like that? It couldn't have been finishing school."

Stunned by the power of her emotion, she couldn't respond. Though she'd been kissed before, many times, she'd never felt such a tempestuous, unbridled desire for a man. And she had no idea how to deal with it.

When he lowered his head and stared at her, Chelsea felt herself drowning in his burning eyes. Vaguely, she remembered he'd asked her a question. "I, uh, I don't know."

Her eyes were hazy, heavy with arousal, her lips moist and red from their kisses. She wasn't quite as naive as he'd thought. That angelic appearance hid a woman with earthly desires and needs. Panicking at the force of his own hunger, Jake did what men have done since the beginning of time. He blamed her for it. If she weren't so tempting, he could have held off. She'd probably had years of practice developing the ability to bring a man to his knees.

A cynical expression crossed his face as he shifted her off his lap. "Don't bother trying to answer that question. I'm sure you've got a list of guys a mile long who've been more than happy to teach you everything you need to know."

She flinched away from him. After exposing herself in such a vulnerable way, he'd cheapened her with that statement. She stiffened her spine. "I believe you've worn out your welcome, Mr. Slater."

He raised a dark eyebrow. "You can drop the mister. We know each other too well for that."

"You force me to be rude," she warned and moved to open the door.

Jake felt relieved and walked to the door. He could handle her coldness much more easily than her passion. "I think we learned something important tonight. Like we mix about as well as gasoline and matches," he said, as much to himself as to her.

He still felt guilty about tricking her with the inventory and couldn't leave without fixing that. "When you come in tomorrow, we'll come up with something a little more meaningful for you to do than inventory."

Still furious and hurt, Chelsea merely gave him a curt nod. She kept her face expressionless as he thanked her for the meal. When she shut the door after him, she let out the breath she'd been holding, inhaling and exhaling deep, cleansing breaths. All the while she told herself that Jake Slater was a rude, egotistical pig she'd like to see cooked into a Virginia ham.

Spying the plate of apple pie he'd left behind, a new wave of humiliation hit her as she remembered how they'd gotten distracted from dessert. She picked up the plate and scraped it. Then, giving in to her fury, she smashed it against the side of the sink.

The next morning, wearing her indignation like a shield, she walked into Jake's office determined to remain businesslike and firm. "Jake, I'd like to start working on the appearance of the front office and making a more organized place for equipment that's signed out. It seems like we're losing equipment."

Jake pointed to her bandaged hand. "What happened to your hand?"

"Nothing serious, just a little accident." Chelsea dismissed his concern and continued. "I'll need help with some of the heavier equipment when it's returned, so if you could assign someone to help me at those times, I'd appreciate it." She turned to leave.

"What kind of accident?"

Exasperated, she turned back around. Hadn't he heard a word of what she'd said? "I cut it. Since you haven't responded to my intentions, I'll assume my plan meets with your approval."

"How did you cut it?" He moved from behind his desk and before she knew it, he was beside her reaching for her hand. She ignored the smell of his aftershave, along with the sight of his large hand over her own. But his touch brought an involuntary tingling that flowed through her body. What was he doing touching her after the way he'd acted last night?

She jerked her hand from his and backed into the door. "Jake," she said with deliberate patience that made her southern drawl more pronounced. "I didn't come in here to discuss my hand. Now, are you going to assign someone to help me or not?"

His expression indicated his dissatisfaction with her response. He stared pointedly at her hand and Chelsea responded by remaining silent, with a mild expression etched on her face. Sighing, he placed his hands on his hips. "Go ahead. You can get Jerry if you need help. He's here every day after school."

A hint of uneasiness darkened his eyes. "But don't go wild with changes or I won't know where anything is."

She would have choked before she thanked him, she was still so upset. So she nodded and left the room.

Chelsea glanced down at her bandaged hand and scowled. Her temper had always been the bane of her existence. Although her mother had tried to force Chelsea to suppress it, she'd still had a few flare-ups with negative results. From the time she was born, her mother had conditioned her that a true lady never raised her voice nor did anything physical in anger. When her mother's friend had brought over a son who persisted in pulling the hair out of her favorite doll, five-year-old Chelsea had grabbed the little boy's hair and given it a few good yanks. Her mother had been mortified and sent Chelsea to her room with no dessert.

When the neighborhood kids had teased her about her father deserting her, Chelsea had chased them into the woods and gotten the worst case of poison ivy she'd ever seen.

It had been years since she'd lost her temper. Of course, she couldn't think of anyone who affected her emotions the way Jake did.

She put the disturbing thoughts from her mind and pushed up her sleeves. Chelsea surveyed the small reception area with a critical eye. Stick-on messages and an out-of-date calendar cluttered one of the two old desks. The other desk held blue prints, bidding estimates, and a tempermental coffee maker. The carpet was an ugly mustard color, probably the result of too many dirty work boots crossing it. She guessed the dull gray walls had once been white.

With a new coat of paint, vacumming, and a general straightening, Chelsea predicted the area wouldn't be half bad.

During the next few days, she cleaned, painted, and rearranged. She also became acquainted with Jerry Mendez. He was intensely shy and she found herself searching for ways to draw him out.

At closing time on Friday, she flexed her stiff shoulders and stretched. "Come on, Jerry, let me buy you a Coke."

The thin, dark-eyed youngster appeared reluctant, so Chelsea encouraged him. "I know you're thirsty and I've kept you hopping every minute today."

She slid the change into the machine and offered him a can of soda. She took a long sip of her own and propped herself on a step stool. "So, how long have you been working here?"

"Four months. Mr. Slater and Mr. Collins gave me the job through the community center." He shrugged his shoulders. "I figured since I'd been caught shoplifting before, they wouldn't hire me. But Mr. Slater said he knows all about hard knocks." Jerry gave his first grin. "He also said if I stole anything from him, he'd string me up and toss me out on my, uh, rear."

Chelsea smiled in return. "You're a hard worker. Do you like it here?"

Jerry's eyes brightened. "It's great. I hand over

most of the money to my mom. But Mr. Slater, he treats me like a real employee.''

''Do you have any sisters or brothers?''

''Seven, including Steve. But he's gone more than he's at home.'' He frowned. ''Steve's been at the detention center pretty much for the last year. Ever since he stole that car . . .'' Jerry sighed and left the thought unfinished.

''Your mother must rely on you quite a bit.'' Actually, Chelsea cringed at the weight of responsibility the youngster bore. She knew the family had been deserted by the father.

''Yeah, she works at the clothing factory, but they don't pay too well.'' The despair in his voice wrenched at her heart. ''She works too hard. She cries a lot.''

''I'm sure it helps her to know that you're such a responsible worker. Why, Jake was telling me just the other day that he wouldn't know what to do without you.'' Chelsea stretched the truth a little. ''You've fit in so well.'' Actually, Jake had said he appreciated Jerry's reliability.

''Wow,'' Jerry's eyes glowed with pride. ''Did he really say that about me?''

''Of course he did, why shouldn't he?'' Chelsea glanced at the shadow that shifted in the hall and hoped Jake hadn't overheard the conversation. ''I guess it's time to go. Thank you for all your help this week. You made the painting go faster.''

Jerry smiled shyly. ''Anytime, Miss Collins. You know, in the beginning, I thought you wouldn't fit in here. But I was wrong. You're okay.''

Chelsea squeezed his shoulder. "You're okay, too, Jerry."

After she went home and ate a cold salad for dinner, she found she was still restless with no place to go. She straightened the house. That took all of fifteen minutes. Then she put a load of laundry in the washer and thumbed through a high-fashion magazine she had no need for anymore.

Glancing at the clock, she noticed there was at least a half hour left of daylight. Chelsea put on her tennis shoes and decided to explore Jake's property. She kept her gaze away from Jake's sprawling ranch home. Though she'd enjoy the company of another human being this evening, she wasn't up to another sparring match.

She saw Mo and called out. "Hello there, Mo. Want to join me for an evening stroll?" The dog barked in response and loped alongside her, nuzzling her hand.

Glad for the companionship, she laughed and obliged him, petting his head and rubbing behind his ears.

"Could you use a guide?"

Her heart sped up at the sound of Jake's deep voice and Chelsea almost refused out of pettiness. She took a deep breath and glanced over her shoulder. "Sure, come on along."

Though she felt the familiar urge to fill the silence, she kept her mouth closed and made an effort to enjoy the evening. Of course, it was difficult to focus all her attention on the sunset with such a distracting man beside her. They walked that way for a while, tossing sticks for Mo to fetch until Jake spoke.

He reached for her hand and inspected it. "Is it better?"

A flutter spread through her stomach at his touch. She'd replaced the gauze and tape with two band-aids that morning. "Much," she said and gently pulled her hand away. She could feel his curious gaze on her and fastened her attention on a stand of palm trees in the distance.

"You never told me how you cut it."

"That's right." Chelsea would sooner eat nails than tell him she'd cut it when she'd broken a dish in a fit of temper the night he'd kissed and insulted her. "How many acres do you own, anyway?"

"About fifty." At her surprised expression, he grinned. "Fifty acres of desert."

"That's a lot of dirt and cactus, considering you don't farm or raise animals."

Squinting into the sunset, Jake hooked his thumbs into his belt loops and stopped. "That's true, but it's mine." He shrugged his shoulders. "I like having my own space. I can come here at the end of the day and not have to deal with anyone but Mo."

Chelsea felt, as she often did, as if she were intruding. "Until I came," she said softly.

Looking back around at her, he paused then agreed. "Yeah."

A chill ran over her skin. She crossed her arms over her chest and sighed. She wondered if she should go back to the guest house so he could be alone. Would she always feel like an interloper where Jake was concerned?

He watched her shiver and she thought she heard a note of reluctance in his voice. "It cools off quickly when the sun begins to set. Do you want to go back?"

She shook her head. "In a little bit. I'm all right if I keep moving. Jake, if your solitude is so important to you, how did my dad end up living out here with you?"

When she stumbled over a rock, he steadied her with his hand on her shoulder. "He helped out with the financing. I built the addition onto the warehouse about a year and a half ago. Ed had gotten weaker by then. He couldn't live by himself anymore."

She felt a wave of grief at the image of her ill father. Blinking back tears, she shook her head. "I never even knew he was sick."

"You didn't come," he said, because it still bothered him. Then, sensing her turmoil, he slid his hand down to rest against the small of her back.

Chelsea came to a dead halt and tossed her hair over her shoulder. "He wouldn't let me. I asked him half a dozen times this last year and he always had some excuse. His lawyer told me Dad didn't want me to see him in such a pitiful state."

"Every time I think about it I want to scream at him, but he's not there." She looked directly into Jake's deep eyes. "I feel so cheated. My mother wouldn't let me come for the first eighteen years. And every time I mentioned it in college, she'd line up a trip to Europe. So, who did he have at the end? His daughter? No."

She sighed in exasperation. "My father didn't want me here when he was alive. But for some reason, he wanted me to come after he died." Chelsea grew tired of defending herself and turned back toward the house. "You've pointed out at every opportunity that you think I don't belong here. But I'm not leaving White Bluff, Jake."

She didn't expect him to come with her. He caught her arm and though she was reluctant to face him with tears in her eyes, she realized she couldn't free her arm. His grip was gentle but firm.

When she turned around, he caught his breath at the sight of her. The breeze picked up strands of her hair, whipping it about her face. He could feel her restraint and her grief, and the desire to comfort overrode every other dark emotion in his soul. His eyes softened and he ran a knuckle over her cheeks. "He loved you, Chelsea," Jake assured her in a quiet voice. "As far as Ed Collins was concerned, the sun rose and set on his little Chelsea." The hard line of his lips gentled at the thought of how often he'd resented Ed's love for his daughter.

The tears seeped from her eyelids and Chelsea burrowed her head in his strong chest. His arms went around her of their own accord and they stood that way for several moments until she gathered her composure.

She lifted her watery eyes to his and rubbed at her cheeks self-consciously. He wondered if she knew how utterly adorable she was to him right now with her eyes red from crying and her sophisticated facade wiped away.

Pointing to his shirt, she sniffed. "I got your shirt wet."

"It'll dry." He touched the dampness on his shirt almost in a caress and whistled for Mo. "Let's get you back. It's too cold out here."

When he took her small hand in his, she didn't protest. And Jake didn't try to understand the lightness in his heart. For a man who'd experienced little gentleness in his life, he'd just shown a tenderness he'd never guessed existed in him. Jake felt another protective layer eased away from the fortress surrounding his heart as he glanced down at the woman who had invaded his life. A strange flare of hope lit within.

They reached her door and Chelsea glanced up at him. "Thanks for the walk . . ." she smiled sheepishly, "and the use of your shirt."

Jake's lips slid into a sexy grin. "Anytime, Chelsea."

Her eyes darkened with emotion. She whispered, "See ya tomorrow."

He raised her hand to his lips, and her muffled gasp went straight to his heart. Releasing it, he held her gaze. "Tomorrow." He watched her close the door and wondered what the hell was happening to him.

The man wanted an interview and he wasn't budging until he got it.

Chelsea glanced at the phone ringing off the hook

and motioned for Jerry to answer it. "Sir, if you could leave your phone number with me, I'll get Mr. Slater to call you back. I'm sorry I can't help you right now, but we're terribly busy." That was putting it mildly. Jake was running between two sites dealing with equipment and inspection problems. Since Chelsea had helped unload a delivery this morning, her ankle was starting to tell on her. And it seemed that every salesman in Arizona had dropped by this morning.

"I called before lunch," the middle-aged man said. "I'll just wait till the boss comes back."

Chelsea sighed. She sympathized with him. She really did. Mr. Sowder called in at least twice a week trying to get work. The least she could do, she supposed, was allow him to fill out an employment application. She pulled one from a drawer.

"Mr. Sowder, Jake probably won't be in until tonight. If you fill out this application, then I'll go over it once you finish. That way, when Jake calls you, he'll have a better idea of your qualifications and experience."

Mr. Sowder mumbled his agreement at the same moment Jerry spoke up. "That was Juan at the Taco Haven site. He said he needs a box of one-inch nails. They'll be able to finish ahead of deadline.

Chelsea smiled in delight. "Great!" She had learned that finishing before deadline often meant the contractor received a bonus. And, of course, it didn't hurt the contractor's reputation.

She started to fly out of the office until Mr. Sowder cleared his throat.

"Oh," she said, remembering her promise to go over the man's application. "Jerry, when did Juan say he needed the nails?"

"Within an hour."

Chelsea glanced at her watch and bit her lip, quickly calculating how long it would take to get to the builder's supply and the site. "Well," she drew out the word. "Mr. Sowder's probably almost finished. I can wait a few minutes."

Why was it, she wondered forty-five minutes later as she sped to the site, that when you needed to rush everyone else moved at a snail's pace?

The owner of the builder's supply had locked the door behind her. He was closing up for inventory for the entire weekend. After her own experience with inventory, Chelsea felt genuine sympathy for the employees.

As if it were becoming a natural tendency, Chelsea's thoughts turned to Jake. His image was firmly planted in the back of her mind no matter how busy she was. He'd been so gentle with her the night before. And she'd sensed something else in him when he'd led her back to the guest house. She'd seen a spark of interest in his eyes that lit an answering flame within her. Chelsea smiled at the thought.

Imagine that. After her mother had trailed one polished dandy after another past her without her feeling the slightest interest, Chelsea's head had been completely turned by a dark-eyed desert man who got his hands dirty on a daily basis.

Pulling the car to a stop, Chelsea was surprised to see how quickly Jake's crew had built the new fast-food restaurant. Surrounded by a few of his workers, Jake looked up when she arrived. Her heart fluttered crazily as he walked toward her. Chelsea grabbed the small paper bag and jumped from the car.

"Hi," she said breathlessly. She offered Jake the bag. "Here are the nails. It looks like I got here just in time."

Jake frowned, staring at the bag. "What?"

"One-inch nails. Juan said he needed a box. I picked up two just in case he needed more." She juggled the bag to prove her point.

Jake's frown grew ominous. "You got two boxes of regular nails," he said quietly.

Chelsea's stomach sank. She nodded, wondering what she'd done wrong this time.

Jake closed his eyes and cursed. He rubbed the back of his neck and turned back to the waiting crew. "We got the wrong nails, Juan. I'll go back into town." He glanced at his watch. "Tell everybody to start cleaning up. I should be back in thirty minutes."

Confused, Chelsea broke in, "Wait. Juan specifically said he needed one-inch nails. That's what I got." She trailed after him as he headed for a company truck.

"Pneumatic nails," Jake corrected tersely. "If you'd let Al take calls from the sites like you're supposed to, you might have known that."

"Al wasn't there. He had to go to the other site. Another piece of equipment broke down."

Jake didn't spare her a glance. "Then you should have called me." He jerked open the truck door.

Disappointed, she murmured, "I was trying to help. You've been so busy."

"That's what I am right now. Busy." Jake got in and started the engine.

Chelsea bit her lip. Dread almost prevented her next words. "Uh, Jake, are you going to the builder's supply?"

"Where else?" he asked, and stared at her impatiently.

She stifled the urge to wring her hands. "Well, they're closed," she said in a quiet voice.

"Closed," he repeated.

"Yes. The owner told me they're doing inventory this weekend. They'll be open on Monday."

Jake jerked his head in disgust. "Do you realize how much money you've just cost this company? We could have gotten a sorely needed bonus from this project. Now it's lost because you couldn't keep your pretty little nose out of my business. I told you to transfer site calls to Al or me."

"I didn't take the call. J—" She broke off when she thought of Jerry. He would be terrified if he saw how angry Jake was. Chelsea didn't want Jake yelling at the boy over this.

She cleared her throat. "I'm sorry. We were very busy. If there's a problem, I accept full responsibility."

"We're talking thousands of dollars, little girl."

Her ire rose at his patronizing tone. With dignity, she set her chin. "I said I'm sorry. You seem to forget that I own half of this business. Therefore, my interest and involvement are valid."

Jake's jaw clenched and his eyes gleamed with anger. "Fine," he bit out. "But you told me to treat you like any other employee. If anyone else had done this, I would have fired him or put him on probation. You're on probation. I don't want you anywhere near the phone."

Her throat knotted, and she was appalled to feel a telltale burning in her eyes. He'd been so quick to assume she'd been the cause of the problem. She'd thought he might be softening toward her after last night. Obviously not.

He deserved a scathing reply. He'd get it, she vowed, just as soon as she thought of one. Right now, she concentrated on holding back the tears. She didn't even try to force any words past her emotion-clogged throat. Turning on her heel, she raced from the site.

By the time she reached the front door of the guest house, her head was throbbing and her eyes burned from crying. She gave an absent little pat to Mo when he whimpered next to her. After tossing her keys on the counter, she slumped into a chair in the den.

Why was Jake so hostile toward her? And why was she so fascinated by him, in spite of that hostility? The thought crossed her mind that perhaps she'd be better off going back to Richmond and licking her wounds. Chelsea remembered the parade of suitable men her mother had set her up with and grimaced. They'd all been smooth, polished, handsome, and bland. And modeling had been a lark, a boring lark.

No, she sighed to herself, she'd stay and make a

place for herself here. The community had accepted her. The other employees had more or less accepted her. Jake was the only hold out.

Well, there was nothing she could do about him right now. She stood and winced at the familiar pain in her ankle, the unfamiliar aches throughout her body.

She thought of a soothing solution and smiled.

Since she was out of wine, Chelsea grabbed the old bottle of bourbon she'd found in the back of a cabinet and poured a little into a tall glass. Shrugging, she poured a heftier amount. She added ice and Coke and shed her clothes on the way to the bathroom.

Her former roommate, Jolene, had told her that whenever she had a horrid day she'd take a cruise bath. A cruise bath, Chelsea had learned, consisted of good wine, candles, music, and tons of expensive bubble bath. The combination did marvelous things for tattered nerves and aching muscles.

After she drew a hot bath and lit the candles, Chelsea slid into the tub and hummed along with the soothing saxophone music coming from her Walkman. She sipped the bourbon and Coke and found it less distasteful with each swallow. A lovely languidness invaded her limbs as she leaned her head back on the bath pillow.

Jake cursed his quick temper and accelerated the jeep. Not five minutes after Chelsea had left, Juan uneasily relayed the entire incident to him. After confirming the story with Jerry, Jake felt the hard edge of guilt settle over him.

She'd walked onto the site looking tired but very desirable. He hadn't figured out how she accomplished that. First dread and then anger had passed through her wide blue eyes. When she'd left she'd looked utterly defeated. And if that didn't drive the stake through his heart, then the sight of her favoring her weak ankle did.

She was getting to him.

Jake couldn't let this rest. As much as he hated to admit he was wrong, he knew he'd jumped the gun. Barely giving her an opportunity to explain, he'd chewed her out. He could call someone on the carpet when necessary. But he never deliberately set out to make someone miserable. Well, he'd done a hell of a job this time, if that wounded expression on her face was any indication.

He scowled and jerked the jeep to a stop. He got out and wiped his hands on his slacks as he contemplated how to approach her. Blessed with a number of saguaro cacti on his property, Jake walked over to one and plucked its white bloom. She liked flowers, he remembered.

Jake shook his head at himself. He was completely out of his depth. When had he ever apologized to a woman? For that matter, when had he cared enough to want to apologize?

Frowning at the sight of her open, unlocked door, he knocked and waited. Nothing. He knocked again, louder, and peered in the door. There was still no answer.

He wondered if she was exhibiting a little feminine pique or crying her eyes out in the bedroom. The second image proved too much for him and he entered cautiously. "Chelsea?"

Jake cocked his ear at a human noise coming from the back of the guest house and headed in that direction, alarmed when he saw her clothes discarded on the floor. Panic swept over him. Had someone broken in and . . .

Grimly, he stalked through the empty living area and threw open the bathroom door. The sight before him stopped him cold.

Chelsea lay in a sea of bubbles, her eyes closed in contentment, as she sipped something icy. Scented candles dimly illuminated the small room. And the only visible part of her below her neck was her dainty pink toenails.

Jake's mouth went dry.

Her complexion was rosy from the steam in the room, her hair tousled. And although he couldn't really see her, the mere knowledge that she was completely naked beneath those bubbles made his heart pound like a jackhammer.

She wore headphones, so she hadn't heard him enter the room. Then, all of a sudden, she opened her eyes and stared at him. She calmly removed the headphones and dropped them on the floor. "What are you doing in my bathroom, Jake?"

Jake couldn't think of a single reply as he stood there—half of him praying that those bubbles wouldn't melt before he regained his mental capacities, half of him praying that they would.

FOUR

Chelsea blew a strand of hair away from her face and glared at Jake. "If you've come to yell at me some more, then you can just leave. I don't want to hear it."

She was more than a little peeved with his presence. Her cruise bath had just begun to work its soothing wonders. And the bourbon and Coke loosened her up enough to forget the fact that, except for rapidly diminishing bubbles, the only thing that stood between her naked body and Jake's heated gaze was bath water.

She watched his Adam's apple bob as she waited expectantly. "Well?"

Jake cleared his throat. Twice. "I didn't come to yell." His eyes ran over her shoulders and he took a deep breath. "I think we'd better finish this conversation in the den." Then, as if he had to tear his gaze from her, he turned and left the bathroom.

Chelsea muttered to herself. "If that isn't just like a man. He gets me upset, so I try to console myself with a few creature comforts. Then, he interrupts my bath and orders me out." The bath water had grown tepid anyway, she rationalized, as she dried herself with a big, fluffy white towel. Grabbing her indigo silk kimono from the hook on the back of the door, she pushed her arms into the sleeves and knotted the sash. She didn't bother with a glance in the mirror before she went into the den. She didn't want to know what she looked like.

Still huffing, she found him seated in the den waiting for her. She plopped down on the sofa and crossed her legs. "So, what do you want?"

His eyes darkened and fell to her lips. Then those telling eyes traveled to the full swell of her breasts and down to her hips. By the time he was studying her legs, the light dawned on Chelsea that this man wasn't interested in conversation. Her whole body grew hot under his visual attention. His gaze moved over her like hands and she felt panicky at how much she wanted his touch.

She gave a little cough. "Jake?" Her voice was husky.

At the sound of her voice, he shook his head and rose from the chair. He rubbed the back of his neck. "I talked to Jerry and Juan after you left. Why didn't you tell me Juan gave you the instructions?"

The edge of irritation in his tone drove her to her feet. Though she could hardly claim to be on equal footing with Jake when they stood toe to toe, she felt less intimidated when she wasn't staring at his knees. She pushed an errant lock of hair behind her left ear. "You didn't exactly ask." Chelsea walked to the kitchen, favoring her ankle. "I'm getting something to drink. Do you want anything?"

He noticed the bottle of bourbon on the counter and frowned at her. "How much of that did you drink anyway?"

"A shot." She paused when he quirked his eyebrow. "Or two. I didn't get to finish it," she added defensively. "I was interrupted."

He strode into the small space between the bar and counter and pulled two glasses from the cabinet. "You didn't need to finish it. With your weight, it probably doesn't take more than two or three shots to put you out." Narrowing his eyes, he asked, "Are you sure you only had two shots? Maybe we need some coffee."

Chelsea gasped in indignation. Who did he think he was? She jerked one glass away from him. "I don't need coffee. For that matter, I don't need someone interrupting my bath and telling me how much I should drink. I was doing just fine until you came."

She sighed. With her anger vented, she suddenly felt tired. "Jake, say what you came to say. I'm not up for visitors tonight." She filled her glass with water, added some ice, and retreated to the den, trying to ignore the way his dark eyes bored into her.

He followed, and after running a large hand through his hair, stood directly in front of her. "Would you sit down and stop hovering over me?" she asked waspishly.

He raised another dark eyebrow and surprised her by sitting down beside her on the sofa. "I talked to Jerry and Juan after you left."

"Yes, you mentioned that," she said and put a bit more space between them. His nearness made her aware of her body, aware of her unconfined breasts and her towel-dried skin. His close proximity also made her uncomfortably aware of his broad shoulders and muscular arms and legs. When he sat this close to her, she had an irresistible compulsion to run her fingers through his wavy black hair and to stroke the shadowed edge of his strong jaw.

He watched her closely and by the look in his eyes, she could almost swear he knew what she was thinking. When she realized she'd begun to fiddle with her necklace, she chastised herself for her display of nerves and clasped her hands around the glass.

"You never answered my question. Why didn't you tell me Juan asked you to get the nails?"

She set the glass down. "Because Juan didn't actually ask me. Jerry did. And I didn't want you losing your temper with him when none of it was his fault."

There was a lengthy pause. "I've never lost my temper with Jerry."

"Well, I didn't know that. I just assumed you treat everyone as you do me." Her emotions were close to the surface and an odd little longing rose up within her. Jake seemed protective of Jerry. She wished he cared for her in a special way. A winsome smile crossed her face. "Could you tell me what he has that I don't?"

His eyes raked over her again and he moved closer. "I think it's more a matter of what you've got that Jerry doesn't."

Her mouth went dry at the heat from his gaze. She knew she should probably stand or move away, anything to break the tension that stretched between them. But she couldn't. Spellbound by his deep voice, she felt herself sinking under the power of his soulful black eyes.

He brushed her hair lightly as if he was calming a skittish mare. "Jerry doesn't have angel hair, or eyes the color of the summer sky." Plunging his long fingers through her hair, he released it from the loose topknot.

She turned her cheek into his hand and sighed. His low voice rumbled through her. "Jerry doesn't have your sexy southern drawl." He muttered a curse under his breath and folded her into his arms. "And he doesn't have a body that's probably gonna put me in an early grave."

Then his mouth covered hers and every sane thought left her head. His lips teased and caressed hers, tugging sensuously at her full lower lip. Her heart raced and her mouth parted of its own accord. Jake plunged his marauding tongue throughout her silken depths, inciting her response.

Like a willow in the wind, she molded her body to his, gripping his shoulders fiercely. They broke apart reluctantly, their breaths sounding harsh in the evening silence.

"Lord, you're beautiful." He ran his thumb over her swollen lips. When she touched her tongue to a calloused finger, he swore and the onslaught against her began anew. His hands joined in the exploration this time. While his skillful mouth drew out her response, he measured her waist, counted her ribs, and probed the fullness of her breasts.

He stiffened at the sound of her little moan and pulled away. "What's wrong?" she whispered, confused by his withdrawal.

"Oh, Chelsea." Jake released her and leaned back against the sofa.

Her heart sank at the self-disgust written all over his face. She braced herself for his rejection, but couldn't prevent a plea from escaping her lips. "Please, Jake, don't insult me again. I don't think I could handle it."

He looked incredulous. "Insult you?" Then recognition dawned and they shared an awkward moment as they both remembered the first time he'd kissed her. He exhaled heavily and reached for her hand. "Hell, I'm the one who deserves to be slapped. I couldn't keep my hands off you."

Twining her fingers with his, she felt a surge of relief. "I didn't exactly push you away," she admitted in a low voice.

"No."

His sexy grin made her heart pound, and she cautiously smiled back.

"You're murder on my self-control, Chelsea. If you were anyone else, I'd have had that robe off you so fast your head would spin."

"My head was spinning."

He shook his head and stood with his back to her. Turning around, he stared at her intently. "This isn't going to work."

Confused, she wrinkled her brow. Not going to work? "What do you mean?"

"You living here. You gotta move into town." Pinching the bridge of his nose, he frowned in contemplation. "Why don't you move in with Al's daughter? She probably wouldn't mind having a temporary roommate."

Chelsea felt as if she'd walked in during the middle of act three. "What on earth are you talking about? Why should I move into town when I already have a perfectly suitable place to stay?"

"It's not perfectly suitable."

Her eyes widened at that. "I'd never figured you for a snob, Jake. My father's guest house may be modest, but it meets my needs."

Jake jammed his hands in his pockets in frustration. "That's not what I meant." As he paced back and forth in the tiny area, she grew frustrated with his senseless conversation. She'd much rather be in his arms.

"Then what do you mean?" she demanded.

When his answer came, it astonished her. "Chelsea, if you keep living here, I'm going to take you to bed."

She inhaled quickly, but the air froze in her throat. He was watching her; waiting for her response. Though she found his bald statement more tempting than threatening, she surmised it wouldn't do to let him know that fact. She called on every single one of her finishing-school lessons in poise and stood. "I believe your taking me to bed would require my consent. I don't remember giving it."

When his sensual gaze mocked her, she hastened to continue. "I'll admit I'm somewhat attracted to you." She saw his raised eyebrow and corrected herself, "All right. Strongly attracted. But I see no reason why we can't control this attraction. It's not as if we're animals."

"You'd be better off in town."

"I'm not moving."

He shook his head at her naiveté, then reached her in two strides. "Baby, your mommy and daddy aren't around to protect you. And I'm not from your sophisticated country club set." Taking in her mutinous stance and expression, he touched her pouty lips with one rough finger. "It's on your head, little girl. Don't say I didn't warn you." Then he turned and left.

Collapsing on the sofa, Chelsea ran shaky fingers over lips that felt as if they'd been singed by his touch. She wondered how one man could turn her knees to jelly with just a look. And wondered just what she was getting herself into.

Over the next few days, Chelsea came to the conclusion that Jake had been exaggerating. She purposely kept her distance, maintaining a polite, businesslike relationship. And Jake seemed willing to do the same. If she missed their earlier conversations, then she put those thoughts aside. A potentially romantic relationship with Jake was just one more item on the list of sacrifices she'd have to make for the sake of her place in her father's business. And from all appearances, it didn't bother Jake if the atmosphere was cooler between the two of them.

She began spending more of her evenings in town with Anita Walker. Al's daughter proved to be sympathetic and fun-loving and soon introduced Chelsea to her crowd of friends. They both shared an interest in the community center. Anita taught English as a foreign language to adults and children.

One evening, after they'd finished their activities at the community center, Anita persuaded Chelsea to visit Rosie's Bar.

"So, what do you think?" Anita's dark eyes sparkled as she led Chelsea into the bar.

Taking in her surroundings, Chelsea struggled for a response. "Umm, it's different."

"I know it's a little rough around the edges, but this is where the cream of the crop of White Bluff's bachelors come," Anita assured her.

Chelsea gave a little smile at that statement. The definition of cream of the crop certainly depended on one's point of view. This establishment was what she'd always termed a man's bar. Dark rough wood panelling held horse-riding equipment and pictures of cowboys. She concealed her grimace at the sight of proudly mounted moose and deer heads. Though she knew it was foolish, she couldn't help her reaction. Every time she saw a stuffed deer, she wondered fleetingly if it was related to Bambi.

Everywhere she looked was wood. Both the tables

and the floor were scarred pine. The scents of cigarette smoke, beer, and hard liquor permeated the air. This was a far cry from the sleek, modern singles' bars she'd occasionally visited in Richmond.

She was so caught up in viewing her surroundings, it took her a couple of minutes to realize how few women were there. She grew a little uneasy at the glances some of the men threw Chelsea and Anita's way. "Anita, are you sure this is a good idea? I don't see many women in here."

Anita waved to a male friend tending the bar. "Of course it's a good idea. Less women mean less competition."

The feeling of unease grew. "What do you mean competition? You're not planning on . . . picking anyone up, are you?" Chelsea couldn't quite conceal her surprise.

Anita laughed. "No, silly. But you have to admit you haven't met many interesting men working at Collins and Slater."

Chelsea could have protested, but thought better of it. "If I'd wanted to meet men, I could have stayed in Richmond," she muttered.

"What?" Anita asked, but then she waved at someone else. "Look, here comes Chris Preston. Most girls would give their eyeteeth for a date with him. He's gorgeous, plus he's a lawyer."

Stifling a sigh, Chelsea looked at the smoothly handsome man and decided her eyeteeth could remain right where they were. The only comforting aspect of seeing Chris Preston again was the fact that he looked as out of place at this primitive bar as she felt.

"Ladies," he nodded his head and greeted both of them. "Chelsea, I'd just about given up hope of ever seeing you again. Where have you been keeping yourself?"

"I've been terribly busy learning about my father's business. And I've spent a fair amount of time at the community center."

Chris brightened at the mention of the charitable cause. "Then perhaps you could be persuaded to help with our upcoming benefit. Several charities join together in a benefit for the community center and awards are given to honor outstanding citizens." He gave a rueful smile. "It's about the only occasion in White Bluff where formal evening attire is required." He chuckled. "Most of the men grumble about it, but the women are holding fast."

Chelsea could imagine some of those grumblings and smiled. "I'd be happy to help. But if this is taking place any time soon, I'm sure most of the arrangements are already made. Please give my name to the person in charge."

"That shouldn't be difficult. My father's the one in charge." After he summoned a waitress to order their drinks, Chris and Anita shared some of their experiences with Arizona's famous flash floods. They soon had Chelsea forgetting her discomfort about the bar and making plans to attach a life raft to her car in case of emergency.

"How long were you stranded?" Chelsea asked Chris in response to his exaggerated tale.

"Oh, forever," he quipped. "I was stuck on the roof of my car for a good hour at least." Then he explained, "The floods don't last very long. But they're dangerous because they occur without much warning."

"I'll bear that in mind." Chelsea sipped her wine and studied the room once more, widening her eyes in surprise when her gaze met Jake's. Dressed in his softball shirt, he smoked a cigarette and stared at her. The man beside him was talking and Jake appeared not to be listening to a word. All his attention was focused on Chelsea and the man beside her.

Suddenly uncomfortable, she gave a little nod and turned back to Anita. Her friend was inquiring about a recent rash of car thefts. "Do they have any idea who's responsible?" Anita asked Chris.

Chris's carefree expression grew solemn, and Chelsea could see that he took his job seriously. "I can't disclose that information. But I can tell you that it looks like amateurs, maybe teenagers."

Both of the women murmured what a shame it was. After twenty minutes more, Chelsea took the opportunity to suggest they leave. She could still feel Jake's gaze on her and, though she couldn't imagine why, he'd looked displeased.

"It was nice seeing you again, Chris," Chelsea said as she hooked her purse over her shoulder.

"My pleasure." He rose and appeared reluctant for her departure. "I'll give you a call about the benefit. Perhaps we can arrange a dinner date at the same time."

"Thank you," she murmured noncommittally. Chris

was nice and handsome. Spending time with him would probably soothe her damaged ego. But Chris reminded her too much of the men her mother had forced on her.

Shaking their heads and smiling at the invitations tossed from several of the male patrons, Chelsea and Anita finally made their way out the door.

Anita grinned and pushed a short dark lock behind her ear. "Was I right? From the way Chris Preston was looking at you, you won't be stuck out in the boonies all alone anymore."

"It's not that far. Besides, I'm not all alone. Jake lives just a few steps away."

"Right," Anita said sarcastically. "You might as well live on the moon with old stone face as your neighbor."

Chelsea's jaw dropped. She'd thought Jake's distant attitude was only directed at herself. "Stone face?"

With exaggerated patience, Anita explained, "Surely you've noticed that your business partner's disposition could rival the coldest day in Antarctica."

Actually, if truth were told, when Chelsea thought of Jake, she remembered the heat of his kiss. She unlocked her car door.

"He must be terrible to work with," Anita said.

Chelsea hesitated to reply. Part of her agreed, but for some insane reason, part of her felt she should defend Jake. Just as she was about to answer, a deep male voice greeted them from behind.

"Ladies," Jake said with a brief nod to each of them.

She was thankful for the cover of darkness because she was sure her face was bright red with embarrassment. Had Jake heard them discussing him? That was all she needed.

Apparently Anita was embarrassed, too. Her new friend shifted her feet and stammered out a combination greeting-farewell. "Oh, uh, N . . . Jake, it's great to see you. Listen, I've gotta go. Give me a call about tomorrow night, Chelsea."

And off the petite woman ran, leaving Chelsea to face stone face. Chelsea pursed her lips to prevent a smile at the unflattering description. She sobered abruptly at the sight of Jake's tight jaw and hard eyes. If his expression was any indication of his mood, she held no interest in what he planned to say to her. So Chelsea opened her car door and feigned a yawn. "It's late. I guess I'll see you tomorrow at work, Jake. Enjoy your evening."

When she turned to step into her car, a large hand fastened securely on her arm in a gesture designated to detain her. She glared at him.

"What were you doing at Rosie's?"

Puzzled, Chelsea knitted her brows. "Anita invited me to stop by after we finished our classes. She's been showing me around White Bluff and introducing me to her friends. Why?"

"You don't belong in a place like that." There was no give in his voice or facial expression, and Chelsea felt a ripple of annoyance run through her. But before she could reply, he continued in that velvet-and-steel voice of his. "Your parents would never approve of you parading through a bar to meet men.''

With studied nonchalance, she made a tsking sound. "You're not being consistent. You've told me at almost every opportunity to get out of your hair. I'm only following your advice by spending time with Anita and other people.''

"I didn't suggest you go out barhopping. Don't you realize that your kind of woman doesn't show up at bars like that?''

He was getting in deeper with each word. She'd been irritated, but the way he kept pointing out how she didn't belong was like rubbing salt into an open wound. "Perhaps I'm turning over a new leaf," she said flippantly. "Just think of it as a change in my image.'' She couldn't resist goading him further. "You know, sweet innocent transformed into brazen hussy.'' The notion was so ridiculous she almost laughed.

Jake cursed and drew her closer to his hard, powerful body. She supposed she should have been frightened. After all, over two hundred pounds of infuriated male held her securely in his arms while his face wore a murderous expression. But she wasn't.

The way his calloused thumb idly stroked the inside of her wrist made her feel faintly weak with arousal. She identified the sharp longing with no difficulty. With Jake, she'd felt it with increasing frequency since she'd met him. But if she didn't want to end up feeling like a complete fool at the end of the conversation, she'd better move away from him.

When she pushed against him, he loosened his grip slightly. "You need a keeper," he muttered.

"That may be so," she conceded and pulled herself the rest of the way from him. She needed the distance to clear her mind. "But if I need a keeper, I'll choose my own. There's nothing in Dad's will to suggest that you need to watch over me." She stared at him pointedly. "That should relieve your mind."

Longing, concern, and anger all warred for dominance on his face. "Stay away from Rosie's," he warned her gruffly.

The trace of longing she glimpsed in his eyes almost did her in until she heard the echo of his. "You don't belong here" in her mind." Chelsea swung into the car and threw his statement right back at him. "I'm not your concern, Jake." Though she wondered if it was a lie, she didn't give him an opportunity to reply. Closing the door, she started her car and left the parking lot. She didn't have to check her rearview mirror to know he watched her. She felt it.

That night, as she lay in bed, Chelsea tossed and turned. Thoughts of Jake and her father battled in her mind. Why had her father left her such a large share of his business? Why had the will stipulated her involvement in the business for a year before she could sell it? And why was Jake fighting her every step of the way?

Hours later, she groaned in surrender to her insomnia and padded out of the bedroom into the kitchen. After pouring herself a glass of milk, she stared out the window at Jake's darkened house. One o'clock in the morning. She gave a self-derisive smile. Jake didn't seem to be suffering from the words they'd exchanged earlier in the evening.

Despite evidence to the contrary, she knew he had a conscience. After all, he'd almost apologized to her twice. Perhaps his gruff manner merely hid a desire to protect her? Chelsea shook her head at that bit of fantasy. No, Jake Slater had made it perfectly clear he wanted her out of his business and out of his life.

"That's too bad, Mr. Slater," she whispered into the darkness. Chelsea tossed the rest of the milk down the drain. She had a feeling Jake Slater could provide her with some of the answers to her questions. If she could just get him to open up.

Surprisingly, she felt better, more relaxed. She walked back to her bedroom and sank into the mattress. Closing her eyes, she resolved to get the boxes of her father's personal items from Jake tomorrow. The last image dancing through her mind before she fell to sleep was of Jake, not frowning, but smiling and holding her in his arms.

But in reality, Jake was frowning.

Moonlight spilled across the exercise room as he pumped his strong legs on the stationary bicycle. The only sounds were the whir of the wheels and his increasingly labored breathing. The classical music he'd put on his compact disc player had gone off. Though the tension was set on its highest level, and though he'd been pumping for a good hour, still he pushed himself.

Forty-six weeks to go, he thought. The will required Chelsea to remain active within the business for one year and she'd been here for six weeks. The vision of her silky hair and flashing blue eyes passed through his mind and he groaned in protest. He'd considered Ed Collins his best friend and mentor. But Jake grew less certain about the future of his sanity if Chelsea continued to torment his days and nights.

Maybe he just needed a woman. It had been a long time since he'd sought the company of the gentler sex. Between the business and Ed's illness and death, Jake simply hadn't had the time.

He finally slowed his pace, cooling down gradually. Maybe he ought to call that redhead at the Bluejay Diner. What was her name? Bobbie, Barbie, Bunny? He shook his head. Jake experienced the sinking sensation that another woman wouldn't do.

Chelsea was getting under his skin.

Grimacing at the thought, he stopped and wiped his face with the towel around his neck.

The window beckoned him and he left the cycle to gaze at his land. What could Ed Collins have been thinking when he arranged his will this way? Jake toiled over the possibilities. He couldn't believe Ed had intended for Jake to watch over Chelsea in a brotherly fashion. Considering Jake's attraction to her, that would be like asking the fox to guard the hen house.

Still, Jake's conscience wouldn't permit him to allow Chelsea to continue on her present course. A hoarse chuckle escaped his throat. *As if he had much control over her actions.* Grimacing at the memory of her in Rosie's, his mind turned over the possibilities. He'd have to be careful. But maybe he could find a way to keep her out of trouble without interrupting his schedule too much. He'd rest easier if he knew where she was most of the time. The tension in his shoulders eased.

Jake glanced at the pocket watch he'd placed on the window sill. Two o'clock in the morning. He was finally ready for bed.

The next day, Chelsea and Jake kept their distance, sneaking furtive glances when each thought the other wasn't looking. Chelsea busied herself with studying the bidding process throughout the morning. She found herself growing more comfortable with shop talk with each new day. She skipped lunch to field phone calls for Jake and was just about to grab a pack of crackers and a Coke when Jake called her.

"I need to see you in my office," Jake said. His deep voice held a tinge of impatience.

That tone of voice never failed to provoke a feeling of apprehension within her. She braced herself, wondering what her latest crime was. But she was tired of being put on the defensive for every imagined offense and she had a few grievances of her own that needed to be addressed.

She found him holding the door open. His gaze instantly surveyed her from head to toe, then swung back to meet her eyes. That annoyed her. The way his large frame loomed over her smaller, more delicate figure annoyed her. But what annoyed her most was her reaction to him. Her heart turned over at the appraising glint in his dark eyes.

Forcing his gaze away from her, he picked up a

piece of paper from his desk. "Why are we getting a bill from Trader Bill's Printing Company?" Jake narrowed his eyes. "You didn't order stationery, did you?"

Chelsea just barely restrained herself from kicking him. "No, the bill isn't for stationery. Perhaps you recall the new magnetic signs we've begun using on the company vehicles."

"Yeah, that's right." He paused thoughtfully, then met her gaze. "That was a good idea. I wouldn't have thought of it."

Stunned by his grudging praise, Chelsea stood silent for a moment. Then she gathered her wits. "Well, thank you. I have some other ideas about some new projects. And I'd like a key to the office if I want to come in early or stay late at some point." She watched him frown and saw a battle warring within him.

"I don't think it's a good idea for you to be here by yourself at night." When she started to protest, he said, "I'll tell you what, if you agree to have someone with you when you decide to stay late, I'll give you a key."

His answer wasn't all she hoped for, but it was a step in the right direction. "I agree. Now, about the new projects."

Jake looked skeptical. But a light flickered in his eyes and his expression cleared. Crossing his arms over his chest, he leaned against his desk. "I'll discuss your ideas if you'll do something for me."

Momentarily distracted by the light in his expressive eyes, she just stared. When he looked at her that way, there wasn't much she wouldn't do for him. His eyes crinkled in amusement. She shook herself, disgusted at how easily she could be swayed by him. "What do you have in mind?"

"Several men go down to the playing field once a week and join the kids from the community center in a game of softball. Our scorekeeper's out sick. Think you could fill in?"

When she didn't immediately respond, he asked, "You do know the difference between an out and a run, don't you?"

FIVE

Although his tone held wry amusement, Chelsea chafed at his implication. "Yes, I know what outs and runs are. I can even identify a strike and a foul," she drawled. She gazed at him with suspicion. "But if you're so concerned about my ignorance, why don't you ask someone else to do it?"

"Nobody else can do it," he responded cheerfully. "Besides, since you've become so involved with the community center, I thought you'd like to see another aspect of it. But if you've got other plans . . ." His voice trailed off and he shrugged.

Chelsea found it less than flattering that he'd only asked her because he couldn't find anyone else. But the opportunity to watch Jake in a different setting was too tempting to resist. Her alternative plans involved going to a party with Anita. Chelsea had to confess, if only to herself, she found the prospect less than appealing. "I'll do it," she capitulated. "What time and where?"

Jake smiled in response. "We'll leave right after work. You may as well ride with me." He stroked his chin thoughtfully. "If you want, we could pick up something to eat on the way home. We won't have time until afterwards," he explained.

"That's fine," Chelsea said and decided to buy some more crackers.

Jake pulled out the gold pocket watch and checked the time. Chelsea was struck by the familiarity of the timepiece, but before she could ask about it, he shoved it back in and said, "Quitting time's soon. We can leave in about forty-five minutes."

He stood and the distance between them decreased. Chelsea felt the corresponding increase in her pulse. She stepped back and nodded. "See you then."

Grabbing her hand, he loosely linked his fingers through hers. His eyes were sincere and his voice could have made her melt. "I appreciate this, Chelsea."

Staring at his mouth, she found herself wishing he would kiss her. Embarrassed by her thoughts, she flushed and pulled her hand away. "It's nothing," she said, her voice husky. She ignored his inquisitive gaze and made her way to the door, saying, "I've got a few things to wrap up. I'll see you in a little while."

An hour later, a little more composed, Chelsea joined Jake for the ride to the playing field. She tried very hard not to think about how close together they were. But it seemed that every move he made—his large hand shifting the gear, the way his thigh flexed when he braked or accelerated, even the way he drummed his long fingers on the steering wheel when they paused at a stoplight—was designed to keep her aware of him and his effect on her. When they reached the field, Chelsea heaved a sigh of relief and sprang from the jeep.

Jake rose from the vehicle at a slower rate while gazing curiously at Chelsea. "I'll introduce you around. Then we'll set you up at a card table with score sheets."

"What ages are the kids who will be playing today?" she asked, looking at the rough playing field.

"Mostly elementary school age. A few of the kids are in middle school." He grinned wryly. "Playing softball with little kids isn't considered a socially acceptable activity for high school guys. Of course, they show up every time we play so they can tell us what we're doing wrong."

Chelsea slit her eyes in amusement. "Oh, I don't know," she drawled, "I imagine the high school kids come because they're in awe of your ability."

He gave a low masculine chuckle and allowed his gaze to run freely over her. "They'll be here," he assured her. "I'm sure they'll want to introduce themselves to you. Just don't encourage them. If they give you any trouble, let me know."

She rolled her eyes at his back and followed him to the benches. The difference between this playing field and the other one she'd seen was amazing. No bleachers lined the perimeter of the field, only a few wooden benches. The diamond was free of vegetation, but tall weeds and stones liberally dotted the outfield. There was also no fence behind the batting area. She wondered how expensive it would be to make the necessary repairs, but Jake interrupted her thoughts with introductions to the other volunteers. All four of the men welcomed her.

Jake found a place for her and one of the other men set up a card table. When the kids arrived, the men divided them up into teams and began to play. Keeping track of each player's batting statistics along with the score kept her so busy she barely noticed how quickly the time passed.

She watched Jake with no attempt to hide her burning curiosity. There was no need to sneak her observations because he was so involved with the children. He coaxed a shy and awkward eight year old into batting. When the youngster reached first base, her heart soared with the triumph shining from both Jake and the little boy's face. He consoled the children who didn't fare so well by patting them on the shoulder, tousling their hair, or whispering words of encouragement. And Chelsea could tell by the way the children responded to him that his attentions were very important to them.

A wolf whistle dragged her attention away and she looked to the side of the field, locating the source of the noise. A group of teenage boys nudged each other, laughing and strutting along the sidelines. She bit her mouth to keep from laughing, and turned back to the game.

Ignoring their catcalls, she kept score until she felt a hand on her arm and warm breath on her neck. Startled, she jerked at the unfamiliar voice.

"Hey, little fox, why don't you leave the babies behind and come out with the big boys?"

Chelsea raised her brows. This guy was bigger and older looking than the rest of the group he was with. He was tall, with long black hair and hard, leering eyes. She was just about to give a freezing rejoinder when she noticed that the youth looked familiar. Something about his bone structure and coloring. "Jerry," she said. "Are you related to Jerry Mendez?"

He frowned suspiciously and backed away. "What's it to you?"

"I work with Jerry at Collins and Slater." Chelsea shrugged and noticed break time was called. "You look familiar."

He hooked his thumbs into his jean pockets with studied carelessness. "Jerry's my brother. I'm Steve." His eyes traveled over her in lustful assessment. "If you like Jerry, you'll like me even better. I can show a woman like you a good time."

Chelsea's lips parted in astonishment. The difference in the two brothers' attitudes was amazing. While Jerry showed her nothing but respect, Steve didn't seem to know the meaning of the word. She shook her head at his suggestion and was about to speak when she felt a heavy, familiar hand on her shoulder.

"Not if you value your life," Jake replied to

Steve. He placed his other hand on her shoulder and favored the younger man with a menacing look.

Steve obviously didn't want to lose face with his buddies who were watching with great interest. But the youth could see he was outmatched. Jake stood at least six inches taller and Chelsea would guess he weighed over fifty pounds more. Fifty pounds of pure muscle, she surmised, by the grip Jake had on her.

Steve shrugged and backed down. "Hey, I didn't see a ring. If she's your woman, you'd better keep an eye on her." Then he grinned insolently and sauntered away.

"What did you do? Invite him over for tea?" Jake asked, censure in his voice.

Insulted, Chelsea tipped up her chin. "Of course not. I ignored their whistles and catcalls. When Steve came up behind me, I noticed his resemblance to Jerry and asked about it. When he persisted with his uh, efforts, I was just about to tell him to leave." She glared at him. "But you threatened him before I had an opportunity. And if you don't loosen your grip on my shoulders, I'm going to have some interesting black-and-blue marks tomorrow."

His hands released her shoulders as if they'd been burned. "Sorry," he mumbled. Taking a deep, cleansing breath, he looked away. "They shouldn't bother you anymore. We take a refreshment break after the fifth inning. You want some lemonade?"

Gazing at him curiously, she noted the clenching of his jaw. She touched his forearm lightly and smiled. "Thank you. I'd love some."

He looked down at her pale hand against his

tanned, muscled arm and rubbed a calloused thumb over her knuckles. She shivered in response. He glanced up at her tiny movement, his eyes darkening with the awareness between them. Reluctantly, he released her hand. "I'll get your lemonade."

When Jake returned, Chelsea's attention was focused on a nine-year-old charmer who wanted a copy of his statistics. Then the game resumed and Jake was coerced into taking a turn at bat.

He played around with the first two pitches, earning a foul and a strike. But then his stance altered; he crouched down and gripped the bat tighter. Distracted by a heckler on the other team, Chelsea missed the next play before it was too late. Someone yelled, "Heads up!"

Instinctively, she raised her head, just in time for the ball to hit her in the eye. "Oh!" she cried, jerking and falling backward to the ground.

The pain was blinding. She clutched her face and rolled to her side, uncaring that she lay in the dirt. "Oh, God." The pounding permeated her face and head so that she barely heard Jake's voice or felt him touch her shoulder.

"Chelsea." His voice came to her, cutting through her pain.

When she failed to respond, his voice roughened with apprehension. "Chelsea, sweetheart. Let me see."

Turning her coiled body into his strong arms, she said, "Jake, it hurts so bad."

"Let me see your eye." He reached to push her hands from her eye.

"No!"

Jake cursed under his breath. "C'mon, Chelsea. Let me see how bad you're hurt."

She peeked out of her uninjured eye. "I already told you it hurts bad."

His lips twitched. "I still need to see it."

Expelling a shaky breath, she removed her hands. She bit her lip but was unable to prevent the tear streaming from her already swollen eye. He cursed again and called tersely to the crowd around them. "Get some ice. I'm taking her to the doctor."

Before she knew it, he swung her up in his arms and into the jeep with some ice wrapped in a cloth held to her. He started the car and spun out of the parking lot.

The pain eased to a steady throb, allowing her to catch a glimpse of Jake's dark expression. Chelsea wondered why he looked so furious, but she held her tongue and concentrated on holding the ice pack on her eye.

They reached the extended hours clinic in record time. Luckily, the waiting room was empty. Jake shuffled her into the doctor and later back out to the car. The kindly old man had informed her she would have an impressive shiner, but her vision shouldn't be impaired. He recommended cold compresses for the first twenty-four hours for both her eye and the back of her head, which she'd hit when she'd fallen backward. The painkiller he'd given her was already making her woozy.

With the worst of the excitement over, Chelsea suddenly felt tired. And hungry. Her stomach growled and she stole another glance at Jake. His expression was still thunderous, but she was past being concerned with his moods. "I'm hungry," she stated baldly.

"What?"

"I said I'm hungry. I haven't had anything but crackers since breakfast. You promised you'd feed me after the game."

He nodded slowly. "Okay. What do you want?"

She relaxed and slumped down in the seat. "The messiest double cheeseburger money can buy. A large order of french fries and a large strawberry shake. Strawberry's my favorite," she murmured. She probably wouldn't be able to finish it, but she figured if she died trying, she'd at least be spared the pain in her head. She closed her eyes.

She didn't open them again until after Jake had bought the take-out meal from a drive-through window and they had arrived home. He took her arm and guided them both through the guest house door. Chelsea immediately relieved him of the milkshake. She sipped strongly on it as if it were her first nourishment in weeks. "Ah," she smacked her lips in satisfaction. "I knew there were some benefits to getting out of the modeling business."

Slumping down on the bar stool, she unwrapped her food and was just about to eat until she noticed that Jake stood there in her kitchen just watching her with a dark expression on his face. She paused and attempted to lighten the curiously strained atmosphere between them. With a straight face, she stared at him through her good eye. "Jake, I realize you've been itching to punch me since I set foot in the office, but I really think a black eye is going a bit far.''

His face was both guilty and incredulous at the same time. He seemed lost for words. "You, you," he sputtered, "you don't mean that."

Chelsea parted her lips in astonishment. She'd expected silence or a snappy comeback. Anything but the sight of stone face losing his composure by sputtering. The irony of it struck her fully and even though her head felt like ten little Indians were beating their drums inside it, she laughed.

"You should see how guilty you look. It makes me wonder just what kind of physical harm you've fantasized doing to me." She saw his eyes take on a strange glint at her comment.

"You're wrong," he said. "Are you going to eat?"

Chelsea sighed and looked back at the food. "Yes, I guess I am."

He reached a strong hand over to cup her chin. "I'd give just about anything to have been able to stop that ball from hurting you." His eyes were full of anguish.

Her heart reached out to him. She understood guilt. She understood it enough to want to relieve him of his. "It's not your fault, Jake." She laced her fingers through his. "If I hadn't taken that heads up' I heard literally, the ball would have missed me." She smiled tiredly. "Lord knows you've wanted to brain me a few times since I've been here, but I don't think you would go this far."

His big body fairly quivered with the release of his breath. "Chelsea, I don't want to brain you. You've tried my patience. But you've become too important to . . . all of us to let anything hurt you." His eyes glowing with hot emotion, he brought her hand to his lips and kissed it. She felt the effects of that touch to her toes.

He cleared his throat self-consciously and released her hand. "Let's go ahead and eat. You need to get to bed."

The following afternoon, Chelsea found herself wishing she'd balked more effectively against Jake's insistence that she take the day off to rest, even though she'd slept until the decadent hour of eleven o'clock. She calculated it had been about six weeks since she'd slept so late on a Saturday morning.

So she indulged in a lengthy bath while giving both her hair and face conditioning treatments, gingerly avoiding her injured eye. She even manicured her toenails and fingernails, a task that grew increasingly superfluous with each passing day she spent in her new career.

By mid-afternoon, she was bored and restless. A vague unease settled in the back of her mind. It was the kind of feeling that made a person even more unsettled because you couldn't put your finger on it.

Shrugging her shoulders in dismissal, Chelsea flipped on the kitchen radio and flopped into the beige chair in the den. Her mouth quirked at the sound of the country music singer's forlorn voice wailing about ex-wives living in Texas. White Bluff, Arizona, certainly didn't lack western flavor.

After the song faded, however, the announcer's voice filled the air with a local retail advertisement. Chelsea stiffened, suddenly realizing where the nagging unease originated.

It was mid-June. She'd known this day was coming. She just hadn't expected to feel so utterly blindsided by the pain. Though she'd sent her step-father an appropriate card and sterling silver pen over a week ago, she'd ruthlessly shoved aside the melancholy she'd felt over losing her own father.

But the time for grief had arrived, and it had arrived with a vengeance. Chelsea finally had to face the fact that Ed Collins was gone.

Tomorrow, people all over America would be celebrating Father's Day. And Chelsea's daddy was dead.

Taking a deep breath, she walked to the hall closet where Jake had stowed the boxes containing her father's personal effects.

She opened the first one and smiled. Bowling trophies and programs from professional baseball games. This was vintage Ed Collins. The man had possessed an obsession for anything baseball. She almost dismissed the programs until she noticed that several bore signatures of famous players. After she searched her mind for what to do with them, she decided to ask Jake. He probably knew someone whose interest in baseball was comparable to her father's.

Setting the first box aside, she moved on to the second one. This one was a little tougher. A lump rose in her throat as she opened the photo albums. Oodles of baby pictures of Chelsea adorned the pages. They were worn and frayed around the edges as if they'd been handled many times. Pictures of Chelsea with her mother, Chelsea in the bathtub.

The black-and-white shot that brought a burning sensation to her eyes showed Chelsea in a ruffly pinafore with what looked like chocolate ice cream all over it and her face. A gleeful smile graced the two-year-old's face as she rubbed noses with her big strong daddy who held her in his arms. Ed's mouth was stretched into a big grin, his eyes adored the tousled urchin. He seemed totally uncaring of the fact that she'd smeared him with ice cream.

This was the father she remembered. Humble, attentive, adoring; but never close enough.

She noted the gap in the sequence of pictures. Ed had left for Arizona when Chelsea was three, begging Vivien to go with him. But her mother had refused, unwilling to uproot herself from her family. For two years, Chelsea had experienced little contact with her father. After that time, she began to see him for two weeks each summer when he'd come to visit her.

The pictures revealed a side of her father she'd never seen. Chelsea's face was predominantly featured throughout the photo albums. Still, there were other people. She saw Al and his family, and some of the construction workers. But of most interest to her were the pictures of Jake. The tough-looking youth with the vulnerable eyes in the photos had grown into a confident man. She even saw a few pictures of Jake with women and wondered at the envy she felt.

With trembling fingers, she carefully placed the photo albums back into the box and moved to the last container. Her breath caught in her throat. She covered her mouth at the sight before her. Letters and letters and letters. Some were written in the careful childish scrawl of a first grader. Others in the elaborate hand of a teenager. Still others fashioned in the hand of a devoted adult.

All the letters were written by Chelsea.

She cried. Until this moment, she'd never really known how important she was to her father. And her heart rent in two that she'd only come to realize it after he'd died. Had anyone ever cared this much for her? Certainly her mother cared, but Chelsea sensed Vivien's disappointment in her as a daughter, as a dancer, as a model. She'd never quite measured up to her mother's expectations.

The tears grew in intensity when she thought of how she'd been deprived from knowing this man who had loved her so. The agony of her loss was so great it was physical. It stole her breath and pierced her soul. She lost her careful control, hugging her knees to her chest there on the floor of her den, heaving great sobs at the injustice of her separation from her father.

An hour later, that was how Jake found her. He said nothing for a moment, summing up the situation quickly. It wouldn't take a psychic to see that Chelsea was mourning the loss of her father. Jake could identify with her loss. He'd just gone through it sooner. The way she'd seemed so composed about her father's death had struck him as a little odd. Now he could see that the cruel brunt of Ed's death just hadn't hit her until now. It probably had something to do with the fact that she hadn't seen Ed except for two weeks out of the year, while Jake had seen him every day.

Sighing, he wiped a large hand across his forehead. Uneasily, he wondered what he should do with her. Crying females had never been his specialty. And this wasn't a pretty, delicate cry. The pain she released started in her heart, and Jake had little experience in matters of the heart. He figured this would be a great time for her mother to arrive from Richmond.

Accepting his fate, Jake lifted his eyes to the ceiling as if searching the heavens for help. Then he crouched down and gingerly stroked her light, satiny hair. "Chelsea." He repeated her name several times, but she seemed not to hear him. Frustrated and anxious, he took her into his arms. "Chelsea, you've got to stop. You're going to make yourself sick."

She burrowed her wet face in his chest as if seeking solace. Jake breathed a little easier when her crying gradually slowed from hiccups to a shaky sigh. The pleasure of holding her soft, trembling body wasn't lost on Jake. His heart picked up when she raised her hands to his shoulders, pressing herself into his warmth and strength.

They sat that way for several moments while she regained her composure. His male body grew uncomfortably aware of her tempting femininity, the crush of her breasts against his chest, her sweet breath against his neck. With great restraint, he controlled the urge to take her lips and distract her from her grief. Later he'd feel like a louse for taking advantage of the situation. As soon as she was calm, he assured himself, he'd release her and get the hell out of there.

Just then, she lifted her head and Jake's heart sank to his stomach. Between her tear-stained face and the black eye he'd caused, Jake knew he wouldn't let her stay alone tonight.

"It was too much," she said, swiping at the tears on her face and grimacing when she nudged her sore eye without thinking. Her clouded blue eyes stole his breath. "The pictures, the letters." She shook her head and gulped. "Tomorrow's Father's Day."

"Aw, hell, Chelsea. You shouldn't have been going through this mess today. You should have been resting, painting your nails and doing whatever women do to make themselves feel better."

Chelsea gave him a weak smile. "I did that this morning. Something had been bothering me for a while, but I didn't know what it was." The little smile faded. "Until I heard an advertisement for Father's Day on the radio."

Her eyes grew troubled again when she looked at the box of letters. Jake couldn't stand the pain in her eyes. He stood abruptly and stepped around the boxes, carrying her out of the guest house.

"What are you doing?"

"We're going to my house. You don't need to be

by yourself tonight. Besides, it's late." He leveled a questioning gaze at her, "and I bet you haven't eaten."

"It's dark," she said in a surprised voice as he carried her toward his home. "I hadn't realized it was so late." Then she seemed to realize he was still holding her in his arms. She squirmed against him. "Jake, I really appreciate this, but you don't have to carry me anymore. My legs are fine."

Her legs were better than fine in his opinion. And he had no intention of putting her down. She felt like she belonged right where she was. He savored the sensation of her feminine body against his own and could have moaned.

"Jake," she began again in an insistent tone. But she became instantly diverted when he carried her into his home. She craned her neck to look at the pictures on the wall.

With a measure of reluctance, he released her, placing her on the sofa in the den. "It's very warm," she murmured, commenting on the yellow-and-brown decor.

"What? Are you too hot? I can turn up the air conditioner."

Then she turned her head and smiled at him. "No. I was talking about the decor. The colors you've chosen are warm and cheerful."

"You sound surprised."

She arched a fine eyebrow. "Well, I guess I am. I've always heard that a person's home says a lot about their personality."

He scowled. "And you're saying I'm not warm or cheerful."

She bit her lip to keep from laughing. "If the shoe fits . . ."

"Let me get this straight," he said, unable to resist the challenge in her eyes. He sat beside her and ran his big hand along the back of her neck. "You think I'm depressing and cold, right?" He found the little shiver she gave when he ran his thumb under her chin very gratifying.

Chelsea swallowed visibly. "I, I didn't say cold."

Her lips tempted him. He wanted to kiss her badly, but appeased his desire with a stroke of his thumb against the inviting pink flesh of her mouth. Her lips opened. He shuddered and took a deep breath. Removing his hands from her while he could, he said, "There's a lot you don't know about me. You might be better off if we keep it that way."

He stood and moved to the kitchen. "How would you like a ham sandwich? I stayed late at the office to do some paperwork so I grabbed another burger on the way home. We can get you fed, then off to my bed, and you'll feel like a million bucks tomorrow."

Chelsea gave an audible gulp.

He turned slowly. She was standing with her hands clenched together and a nervous, self-conscious look on her face.

Her words came out in a rush. "Jake, you've been very kind. I truly appreciate your taking care of me when I was so upset. But I'm not ready to," she paused and groped for the right way to say it. "I don't think it would be a good idea for us to . . ."

Jake frowned. "For us to what?"

She rolled her eyes in that do-I-have-to-spell-it-out manner, then looked away. "Go to bed, but thanks for everything, I'll see you tomorrow." She headed for the front door like there was a fire in the house.

And there was, inside of him. But he wasn't taking her to bed tonight. She needed something else from him tonight and even if it killed him, he was going to give it to her.

Following her, he grabbed her shoulders and held firm even when she flinched. The wariness in her gaze when he turned her back around wounded him. "You shouldn't be alone tonight. The grief over your father hit you about as hard as that softball did yesterday." Her eyes widened in surprise. "I'm sleeping on that sofa. You can have the bed." Her shoulders relaxed until he said,

"You're safe. For tonight."

SIX

After Jake put together the thickest ham sandwich she'd ever seen and insisted she eat every bite of it, he all but shoved her into his bedroom and closed the door. She opened it to try once more to persuade him to let her take the couch, but he'd already disappeared.

Sighing, she turned back around and looked at his room. Spacious, sparsely furnished, she noted. The bed was large, like Jake. She could picture him there easily. As a matter-of-fact, she could picture Jake and herself together in that big bed all too easily.

Chelsea groaned. She pushed off her own clothes and pulled on the T-shirt Jake had left on the freshly made bed for her.

Two pictures sat on his dresser, one with a dark-haired young boy and a proud but thin and hollow-eyed woman behind him. Chelsea assumed the

114

woman was his mother and felt a catch in her throat for the little boy Jake had been, for the loss he had experienced with the death of his mother. She remembered the afternoon Al had told her about Jake's past.

The other picture made her smile. Jake held a diploma, while Ed stood with his arm slung across Jake's shoulder. Both men wore triumphant smiles.

Chelsea's smile wavered. Ed had been unable to attend her college graduation. She hadn't known it at the time, but he'd been too ill to travel.

Restlessly, she pushed aside her conflicting feelings and turned down the bed. Just as she was about to turn out the table lamp, she noticed a picture on the wall. It was a pastel drawing of a photograph her father had taken of her. She narrowed her eyes at the picture, remembering the occasion. Fifteen years old and all dressed up in a white dress that complimented both her budding womanhood and girlish innocence. In spite of the fact that he'd probably rather be anywhere else, Ed had taken her to see a traveling ballet troupe that night to please her. The memory of the pride glowing in his eyes brought a lump to her throat.

She swallowed it down. She'd shed enough tears today. It was time for bed. Still, something about that picture bothered her. She looked for a signature and found none. What was Jake doing with this picture? Surely it had belonged to Ed. But why hadn't Ed mentioned it in the will? It seemed logical to Chelsea that Ed would have wanted *her* to have it, not Jake.

She snapped off the lamp and tumbled into bed, brooding. She'd always considered jealousy a useless emotion, always tried to tell herself she was above such pettiness. But Chelsea was feeling low. And as much as she'd like to deny it, she felt jealous of Jake and the relationship he'd shared with her father. It was childish, she chided herself. But she still felt it.

She wished Ed had been there for her graduation. She wished Ed had given her the pastel drawing. She wished she had been the one to care for him when he'd been ill.

Chelsea turned over and thumped the pillow. Might-have-beens serve no purpose, she told herself. Be thankful you had a father who loved you and showed it. And although Jake hadn't always been exactly charming, he'd been achingly tender and kind to her tonight.

She began to relax and thought of Jake. Though the linens and T-shirt were freshly laundered, she smelled him. The last thought that ran through her mind before she drifted off to sleep was that she was surrounded by him.

Surrounded by Jake. The thought was oh, so pleasurable. A dreamy smile crossed her lips.

The next morning Jake pulled the jeep to a stop at the old cemetery. He studied Chelsea carefully, her little pink mouth set in such a tight line, her stiff posture, the way her fist tightly clutched the small bouquet of flowers. "You sure you want to do this?"

Chelsea squared her shoulders and glanced at Jake.

"Yes, and thank you for bringing me. You really didn't have to."

Jake released his seat belt and opened the door. "Yes, I did. I couldn't let you come out here alone."

Taking a deep breath, she left the jeep and joined Jake. When he took her arm, she felt his support, emotionally and physically. She released a little sigh. It wasn't so bad thus far, she thought looking around. Just an old, but somehow peaceful cemetery. The only difference lay in the fact that her father had been put to rest here. "What was the funeral like?"

Thoughtfully, Jake answered, "Simple. That's what Ed stipulated in his will. Near the end, he was always telling me he didn't want people making a big fuss. Al and I made the arrangements with the minister of a local church Ed had attended occasionally."

He stopped for a moment and she asked him, "Did many people come? I guess I mean, did he have many friends at the end?"

His gaze was turbulent with emotion. "The church was packed, Chelsea. Everyone loved Ed Collins. He was a fair businessman, a good friend."

For some reason, she felt the need for Jake to know why she'd been absent even if he condemned her for it. Her attempt at a laugh caught in her throat and she bent her head, staring at the dry earth. "It's crazy, you know. I've only rebelled against my mother a total of three times in my life. The first time was when I moved out and began modeling. My mother was furious." She lifted her head, gazing into the distance. "But furious wouldn't begin to describe what she was when I decided to move out here.''

Chelsea smiled absently. ''I guess that's something you and Vivien would agree on. She said I didn't belong here.''

Chelsea felt him shift, and shook her head. ''Anyway, the other time I rebelled against my mother was the weekend before one of my best friend's wedding. I joined a group of sorority sisters who went up to Atlantic City to gamble and casino hop. It was supposed to be the bride's last hurrah.''

Her voice quivered. He gripped her shoulders. ''When I got back on Monday morning, it was too late.'' She looked into his eyes, tortured with her own guilt. ''I missed my daddy's funeral because I was having a good time playing blackjack and spinning wheels.'' Tears filled her eyes.

Jake's arms enfolded her, squeezing her. She felt his lips on her hair. ''Chelsea, it's okay. He wanted you to remember him when he was healthy.''

''How can you be sure?'' she asked desperately.

''I can't. But that sounds like him. Why else wouldn't he let you come to see him those last two years?''

The statement hung between them with the potential of a healing balm. She accepted it and instantly felt the release of guilt and pain. She looked up into Jake's face, awed by his ability to say just the right thing.

He was becoming so important to her, more important than just a business partner. She touched his cheek and watched his eyes darken with emotion.

Pulling him down, she pressed her lips to his. "Thank you," she whispered. He tightened his arms momentarily, then released her away from his strong body.

They continued to Ed's gravesite where Jake gave her a moment's privacy when she laid down the flowers and remembered her father. With a lighter heart, she walked back to the jeep with him.

Jake pulled a gold watch from his pocket to check the time and with that single gesture the air of peacefulness between them shattered. "It's too late for breakfast and too early for lunch. Is there anywhere you want to go?"

Although she heard his words, they were far from her mind. "That watch," she said. She kicked aside a rock and stumbled in her eagerness to touch the timepiece. "That watch belonged to my father. It belonged to my grandfather."

She saw his hand enclose it more tightly. His face grew wary. A seed of suspicion grew. She couldn't keep the accusing tone from her words. "What are you doing with my father's watch?"

She watched his face close up as tight as the hand holding the watch. He slipped the timepiece into his pocket and answered her in a cold voice. "He gave it to me."

The words were like salt rubbed into an open wound. First the picture, now the watch. "But that watch belonged to my grandfather. My grandmother gave it to him as a gift."

Jake said not a word, opening the door and settling

into the jeep. He glanced at her meaningfully as if to tell her to get in the jeep.

The temperature rising in Chelsea was due to more than the desert heat. "That piece of jewelry is a family heirloom," she continued, putting an emphasis on the word family. When he didn't respond, she blurted, "I can't believe my father gave that watch to you."

By Jake's angry expression, she wondered if she'd gone too far. "Well, I hate to break the news, little princess, but he did." And then, as if his patience had been totally exhausted, he jerked his head to the passenger seat of the jeep. "I don't have all day. It looks like you've recovered from your grief. Get in if you want a ride home. I've got things to do."

A muffled, indignant squeak escaped her lips and she stomped over to her side of the jeep. What she wouldn't give for a ride with anyone else on the planet, Chelsea thought. She plopped herself down on the seat and slammed the door.

Without preamble, Jake started the engine and left the cemetery. Acting as if she weren't there, he lit up one of his cigarettes. He knew how much she hated the habit. Chelsea narrowed her eyes, wondering if he'd done it to annoy her.

She didn't comment. She just opened her window and brooded.

She wanted that watch. It might not be reasonable, but she felt strongly about it. She felt she'd had so little of her father his entire life. The watch represented more than a generation of Collinses. It seemed to Chelsea that she, Ed's only blood offspring, was the rightful owner. When she mentioned her opinion to Jake, he all but laughed in her face.

"Forget it," he said. "If Ed had wanted you to have it, he would have given it to you. Besides, you've got the guest house and the larger share of the business." He looked at her suspiciously. "Better watch it, Chelsea. You're beginning to sound greedy."

Greedy! "I'll buy it from you," she offered desperately, wondering at the same time if she had enough money. "We could get it appraised by a local jeweler. I'd be happy to pay you a fair market price."

"Forget it," he growled. "Money can't buy you everything."

She was about to protest when she watched him viciously squash the cigarette in the ashtray, the gesture telling her more than his too-calm voice. He was furious with her.

That cool, disinterested attitude remained over the next few days. He'd barely spoken to her for the rest of the ride home except to mention his plans to chop down some dead trees on his property.

"You'll probably die of sunstroke if you work in this heat, especially in the middle of the day," Chelsea informed him.

Jake glared at her, then muttered, "I can't get away from the heat no matter where I go."

She would almost swear that remark carried a double meaning, but dismissed it when he continued to act so indifferently toward her.

But Chelsea still wanted that watch. If nothing else, her argument with Jake had helped to refocus her energy. Although she felt a deep ache for the loss of her father, her feelings of frustration over Jake superceded all other emotions.

In spite of the fact that he ignored her, she was still enormously attracted to him in a way she couldn't deny, even to herself. For the first time in her life, Chelsea wanted a man for more than a casual date or friendship. And for all her finishing-school manners and charm, she hadn't the first idea of how to attract a man like Jake. So she put the whole mess on the back burner and put her energy back into the contracting business.

Much to Jake's dismay.

On Monday, she took quite a bit of teasing over her black eye until she explained that it had only been trying to catch a wild hit of Jake's. The teasing turned to Jake where it ceased abruptly due to the dark looks he gave the men.

On Tuesday, Chelsea reminded Jake of his promise to discuss a new project she wanted him to try. At first, he claimed he was too busy. When Chelsea surreptitiously stroked her black eye, he seemed to think better of it and invited her into his office.

"So what do you want to try, Chelsea?" He tilted back in his chair and squinted while taking a draw from his cigarette. His shirt sleeves were pushed up to reveal muscular tanned arms with a sprinkling of dark hair on them.

Chelsea could easily find herself distracted by those strong arms, especially if she remembered how wonderful they felt wrapped around her. But that wouldn't help her case. So she focused on the annoying cigarette instead. "I want us to start building decks."

Jake raised a dark eyebrow skeptically. "Decks?"

"Yes, decks," she said firmly. "We've received a ton of calls from people asking if we install them. It makes sense that we fill that need, especially if the economy remains sluggish. More people will stay home instead of vacationing."

He sat forward, snuffing out his cigarette, and spoke in a patronizing tone guaranteed to drive her straight up the wall. "Chelsea, why should I waste my time on a two-bit deck job when I've got another contract for a doctor's office that will require every man I've got?"

"Because we wouldn't have to use those men. We could hire new people part-time for this. There's been at least four people in here lately just begging for work. Besides, this kind of job could fill the gaps during slow periods. Have you looked at Mr. Sowder's application?"

"Yeah, the guy's a little rusty, but qualified." Jake thought it over for a minute then shook his head. "I'll consider it after we finish the doctor's office."

Chelsea sighed but pushed ahead. After all, he hadn't said no. "Well, have you thought any more about the new bigger signs for the sites. It would be great advertisement and you could use them over and over."

"We don't need them, Chelsea. You forget this is a construction company in a small town." He paused and his eyes trailed her body in a gaze that burned on its way down. "Of course, since your background's in modeling, I wouldn't expect you to know that."

His comment felt like a slap in the face after her attempt to reason with him. Anger and disappointment coursed through her. That beautifully shaped head of his held a mind with a closed steel trapdoor. Though she had no intention of dropping the issue, she gave a docile nod and said in a compliant voice, "As you wish. You're the boss."

Jake narrowed his eyes at her as if he'd expected a fight, questioning her submissive behavior. But Chelsea just thanked him for his time, turned, and left the room.

When she reached the front office, she went directly to the phone. Thankfully, the only person in sight was Jerry Mendez. She dialed the number. Then, with her blood still boiling over Jake's rejection of her suggestion, she calmly placed an order for the signs she'd just discussed with him.

She hung up the phone, her eyes sparkling, her cheeks flushed. A satisfied smile curved her lips. Defiance must be good for the soul.

Jerry interrupted her thoughts. "Uh, Miss Collins, could I ask a favor?"

Chelsea turned to the shy youth shifting his feet, wondering what was troubling him. "Of course," she encouraged, "what can I do for you?"

He checked the doorway to make sure no one was listening. "I have this project in art appreciation I have to do. I gotta pick something to do with art or music and do a project on it." He lifted his hands. "I don't know where to start."

Chelsea's heart turned over at the realization that Jerry trusted her enough to ask for her help. "I'd be honored. And the first place to start is the library. I'll bring a few books of my own so you can select something that interests you. Then we can stay after-hours a few nights to work on it together. When is it due?"

"In six weeks." Jerry looked endearingly hopeful. "You sure you don't mind."

Chelsea smiled her reassurance. "Not at all."

Suddenly, she heard the roar of an engine and the sound of glass breaking outside. Chelsea frowned and looked out the window. It was Steve, Jerry's brother, with a bunch of his buddies in an old Thunderbird. She grimaced at the broken beer bottles the youths had just smashed on the pavement of the parking lot.

She turned at the murmur of distress Jerry made. "Jerry, I know Steve is your brother, but Jake won't like this one bit. I think you'd better make other arrangements for getting home."

Jerry sighed. "I'd rather walk than ride with him." His young face dark with anger, he scowled. "I'm not letting him mess up this job. It's the best thing I've got going." He looked back at her. "He won't be around here again, Miss Collins. I'll make sure."

Chelsea squeezed his shoulder. "Don't worry about the glass. I'll take care of it."

She watched him leave the office, shoulders squared,

as though he carried a heavy burden, and wished she could do more for him. Chelsea felt a deep admiration and respect for the young man. She understood why Jake and her father had allowed him to come to work for the company and was thankful for their insight.

After sweeping up the glass in the parking lot, she brought it in to dispose of it. Al had just finished a telephone call with a distributor. He whistled at all the glass she carried. "Has Jake seen that?"

Chelsea dumped it into a garbage can and shook her head. "No, and I'd rather you not mention it to him. Jerry's brother dumped this in the parking lot and Jerry's going to ask him to stay away. He was pretty upset. So I don't think we need to bring Jake into this."

"He won't hear a word from me," Al assured her. "I like the kid." He shook his head. "But that brother of his is trouble." Al put his hands on his hips in a defiant gesture. "If he comes around again, you tell me. I know how to take care of those kind of punks."

Chelsea bit back a smile at the image of this kind, balding, middle-aged man taking care of a slippery young man like Steve Mendez. "I'll remember that," she said and went on to discuss her plans to join Anita for dinner since both women were teaching at the community center that night.

She met Anita at a fast-food restaurant an hour later. The two women grabbed one of the few available tables in the crowded restaurant. Chelsea slid into her seat and removed her sunglasses.

Anita gasped. "What happened to you?"

Chelsea smiled at the look of horror on her friend's face. She forgot about her injury until someone made a remark about it or she happened to look in the mirror. "I guess I forgot to tell you. Jake asked me to keep score at a softball game and one of his hits went a little wild. I got hit in the eye. He was so upset, he rushed me to a doctor."

Anita looked skeptical. "Stone face was upset? Give me a break, Chelsea."

"He was," Chelsea protested. "After he took me to the doctor, he got some dinner and drove me home." Her cheeks warmed at the memory of the way he'd carried her in his arms. "He said he would have done just about anything to prevent that ball from hitting me."

Anita narrowed her eyes and nibbled a french fry. She cocked her head to one side, studying Chelsea. "That doesn't sound like the Jake I know. Do you two have something going on?"

Chelsea choked on the bite she'd just swallowed. She felt her face flush and hoped Anita would attribute it to her coughing. "No, Jake isn't the least bit interested in me." She couldn't conceal the tinge of disappointment in her voice. "I don't think he sees me as anything more than an annoyance."

Anita snorted. "Then the man is blind. White Bluff doesn't exactly have a surplus of gorgeous blonde ex-models. Jake may not be Casanova material, but he's no monk. To tell you the truth, I don't know much about his love life. He's not one to discuss it."

The question popped out before Chelsea could stop it. "Is he seeing anyone now?"

"I don't think so. He's been pretty busy with the business since your dad died. And he's one to put business first, pleasure second." Anita chewed a bite of burger thoughtfully and took a sip of Coke. "I remember one girl who got too serious. She was talking marriage and he had to end it real quick." She gazed at Chelsea curiously. "Why do you want to know?"

Chelsea gave what she hoped was a convincing shrug. "He's my business partner. It pays to know where his priorities are." Anita nodded and continued talking, but Chelsea was only half listening. So, he wasn't seeing anyone and he was scared of marriage, she thought.

"So how about it?" Anita's voice broke through.

"Pardon?" Chelsea blinked.

Anita repeated with exaggerated patience. "The Chamber of Commerce is having a luncheon where most of the businesses of the area will be represented. The mayor, Randolph Preston, has suggested that a group from the community center be a part of the program. It will help promote the center's benefit that's coming up next month. Do you think one of your dance classes could do it?"

Chelsea's mind clicked into high gear, considering the different possibilities. She felt a tingle of excitement. "I'd have to keep it simple since most of the girls have only taken lessons for several weeks. Two numbers at the most." She gave Anita a broad smile. "I'll do it."

* * *

The next morning, Chelsea woke early as she had for the last several mornings. Mozart barked, and she heard Jake shush him in a low voice through her open window. She glanced at the alarm clock and groaned. Five o'clock in the morning. The man was insane, she fumed as she tunneled back under the covers, intent on catching a few more winks.

Every morning since Father's Day brought Jake bright and early to work on the rotting trees on a far corner of his property. When she'd asked him why he had to do it so early, he'd explained that he chose the morning to escape the heat.

When she woke again at seven, she showered and dressed for work in a gauzy cotton shirt and skirt, with strappy flat sandals. She'd developed her own sense of style over the last few weeks, finding she needn't relinquish her femininity just because she worked in a contractor's office. She just had to be more practical—no more short skirts, silk suits, and spiked heels.

She also found she preferred wearing less makeup, just a bit of blush, mascara, and lip gloss. But she'd never give up her perfume. After spritzing on the floral scent, Chelsea gave a last glance in the mirror and sauntered out the door. She wasn't due at work for an hour, so she saw no need to hurry.

The first thing that jarred her was the sight of Jake's jeep parked in the driveway. She frowned. He never ever went into work late. Since she'd arrived in White Bluff, Jake went to work before everyone else and stayed until dinnertime.

Even Jake needed a vacation day every now and then. Perhaps he'd planned on taking the day off. Just as she moved toward her car, she saw Mozart running so fast he scattered dust in his wake. The dog barked furiously. Had Chelsea not been aware of his affectionate nature, she would have sought refuge.

When he continued his swift speed even though he grew closer, Chelsea braced herself against the side of her car and wondered if he was going to lunge onto her. He stopped directly in front of her, dancing from side to side, his tongue panting from exertion.

"Mozart," she laughed and petted his head. "Have you seen a cat or a jackrabbit?"

The animal didn't respond to her soothing tone. To Chelsea's surprise, he took her skirt between his teeth and tugged. "Hey, cut that out. I don't have that many casual clothes."

But Mozart only whined and tugged her skirt again. Chelsea was dismayed. The dog had never acted this way before. He seemed to want her to follow him. She glanced at her watch and saw she had a few more moments to spare. Perhaps he'd found an injured animal.

Shrugging, Chelsea relented. "All right. Lead on, Mo."

With that, he barked and ran.

"Wait up," she called, wishing she'd worn tennis shoes for this excursion.

After chasing him for close to a mile, Chelsea was covered with perspiration and dirt. Whenever she stopped to rest for a moment, Mozart returned to her, barking and nipping at her skirt again.

She traveled only a few moments more and felt her heart sink at the sound she heard. A pile of heavy logs had been dislodged and tumbled down. Onto Jake.

"Mo." His voice sounded rusty to her ears as he called for his dog. Her pulse pounding in her skull, she raced closer. He was covered from head to toe with the heavy rotting logs.

She choked out his name, "Jake."

He paused and she heard his labored breathing. Had he broken something? Was he delirious? She murmured a prayer of thanks that he was at least conscious.

"Chelsea?" his voice held disbelief.

Her response came out in a rush of words. "Yes, it's me, Jake, what have you done? We've got to get you out. How long have you been under there?"

"Mo was chasing something while I was stacking the logs. Somehow, the brace came undone and the logs fell on me. I don't know how long I've been here, probably a couple of hours. I think I may have cracked some ribs, Chelsea."

She could hear him working to conceal his pain. Tears burned her eyes. "We've got to get you out, Jake." Scrambling to the pile of logs, she tugged and pulled. She couldn't budge them. She tried again and again pushing and pulling.

"Jake, they're too heavy." She pushed back her hair in frustration. "It will take me at least an hour to get someone here to help."

The disappointment and weariness came through in his voice. "Chelsea, go call—"

She cut him off, spying something that would facilitate his release. "Wait!" If she could just operate it properly, Jake would be out in minutes. Her only problem was that she'd never used one before.

"Jake," she said as she lifted the heavy piece of equipment, "tell me how to turn on this chainsaw."

SEVEN

"God help me," muttered Jake in a voice just loud enough for Chelsea to hear.

Knitting her brows, she placed the chainsaw on the ground and rubbed her damp palms over her gauzy skirt. "Jake, it's fine with me if you want to pray. But since we've got this chainsaw, I think we might make a little more headway with those logs if you told me how to start this thing."

His groan sounded pitiful to her ears. Her heart caught at the sound and she wondered if he was in worse condition than he'd first said. "Jake, answer me. Are you conscious?"

"Yes, I'm conscious. I just can't believe my good luck in having you, of all people, rescue me."

That irritated her almost enough to let him lie there and fry for another hour before other help would come. "If you don't mind waiting for another hour or so, I'll be happy to call someone else."

When he paused, her irritation flared to anger and she marched off.

He must have heard her footsteps because he called out, "Wait!"

"Yes?"

"Come back and I'll tell you how to operate the chainsaw." His voice was resigned.

"What's the magic word, Jakey?" she chided him, hoping her impudence would take his mind off his situation.

There was another pause.

"Well?" she prodded.

"Please." he said sullenly.

She smiled and moved back to the saw. He sounded just like a recalcitrant schoolboy.

Then they both became serious. "Always keep the blade pointed away from you," Jake instructed. "And for God's sake, keep it away from me, too."

"I understand, but how do I start it?" she asked, pulling ineffectually on a cord.

"Stand up and brace your foot on the chainsaw. Can you do that?"

Chelsea wiped the perspiration from her face and pushed her limp hair behind her ears. It was so hot she would have traded the Hope Diamond just for a breeze. "I've got it. Now what?"

"Now, take the cord in both hands and quickly pull it all the way out."

Chelsea did that. About ten times. The only thing she'd gotten for her efforts was a weak sputtering sound and the smell of gasoline.

"You flooded it," Jake said.

"Oh!" she exclaimed and kicked the dirt. The sun beat down on her. She no longer cared that her clothes stuck to her so she looked like a limp dishrag. Tears of frustration threatened, but she held them back, taking deep breaths of the still hot air.

"Chelsea," Jake sounded weary. "Are you ready to try again, or do you want to go for help?"

She turned back to the saw, viewing the stubborn machine as a direct challenge to her competence. She sighed and took her position. "I'll try again."

Biting her lip, she silently prayed and jerked with all her might. The saw came to life.

Her eyes widened in astonishment. "I did it," she whispered. "Jake," she shouted, staring at the vibrating saw, "I did it."

"Good girl," he called out. "Now start cutting these logs."

She wiped her palms on her skirt again and ordered a barking Mozart out of range. "Keep talking so I don't get too close."

And talk he did, more than she'd ever heard him talk before. If she hadn't been concentrating so hard on cutting the logs, she would have enjoyed listening to him. As it was, she knew she'd never remember anything he said.

At one point, she felt a sharp stinging sensation on her left arm. She jerked and brushed a small black bug off, wincing at the burning pain.

Finally, she'd sawed enough logs for Jake and her to push the wood aside, freeing him from his trapped position. He was dusty and dirty. His face wore a weary, pained expression. And he'd never looked better to her.

She extended her hand to him. He took it, grimacing as he eased himself to stand. Gingerly, he examined his ribs. Jake grunted, pulling the perspiration sodden T-shirt away from his skin. "I think they're only bruised."

Spotting a scrape on his cheek, Chelsea raised her fingers to it, frowning at the pain she felt radiating up her arm. She pulled back her hand and massaged her arm.

Jake glanced at her. "You're a mess. What's wrong with you?"

"Thank you and likewise," she retorted, feeling unreasonably anxious now that he was free. If her arm hadn't bothered her so much, she'd have been dumbstruck by the overt display of his masculine chest. But it hurt badly, and she just wanted to get back to the house. "If you're all right, I'm going back now."

She turned away, walking stiffly toward home, ignoring his puzzled expression.

"Hey," he called. "Wait up. You're not mad 'cause I told you that you looked like a mess, are you? I mean, hell," he caught up with her, "I probably look like something you dug up out of the ground."

Jake laughed awkwardly. "That was supposed to be a joke, Chelsea."

But Chelsea wasn't laughing. The pain had reached her shoulders by now and her muscles felt as if they moved in great clenching motions. She bit her lip, wondering what had happened to her.

"Chelsea," Jake clasped her arm.

"Don't touch me," she cried, pulling away and running. She was frightened by the enormity of the pain. She ran for several minutes until the cramping became too much. Kneeling on the ground, she held her arms across her abdomen and doubled over.

"Chelsea." Jake's voice was breathless and rough with worry. He stood beside her. "Tell me what is wrong. Did you cut yourself? Have you got a cramp?"

"Yes." The word was wrenched from her lips. "A cramp. All over." Jake was saying something else, but she barely heard, she was so focused on overcoming the pain.

When he lifted her arm, she jerked, but he held firm. He rubbed his fingers over the tiny red marks on her arm. "What's this?"

"Bug bite. It happened when I was using the chainsaw." She began rocking, feeling her control slip away. "Jake," she pleaded.

Jake frowned. "What kind of bug? Was it black with a red spot?"

Why was he asking her these questions when she felt like she was going to die?

He shook her gently. "Chelsea, answer me. It's important."

Maybe if she answered him, he'd take her home. "It was black. A spider. I think it had a red spot." She twitched involuntarily, feeling a wave of nausea.

She clenched her eyes closed, but the tears fell anyway.

Then Jake hauled her up in his arms against his chest. He spoke in a gentle, suffering voice as he strode forward. "You've been bitten by a black widow spider. I've gotta get you to a doctor."

A tidal wave of anxiety and excruciating pain swept her again. "I'm going to die."

"No!" he practically shouted. "You will not die." The sun beat down on them mercilessly. "But you're gonna hurt like hell for the next day or so. The aches, pain, and anxiety are all classic symptoms."

In the recesses of her mind, his words penetrated. A fragile sense of ease emerged, whether it was due to his words or the sensation of his strong arms around her, she didn't know.

They didn't speak. Jake seemed to sense her need to concentrate. She drew deep, difficult breaths, hanging onto his assurance that she would live. Her pain had not lessened. If anything, it had grown more severe, enveloping her in agony.

He carefully set her in the backseat of the jeep, handling her as if she were a priceless treasure. He stroked her head, crooning, "Baby, you'll be okay."

Jake made the trip to the hospital in record time, carrying her into the emergency room without preamble. Before she knew it, her limp clothing was removed from her clammy skin and an intravenous solution with painkillers and muscle relaxants was flowing through her system.

Hours passed in a haze of pain and semi-consciousness. Her body and mind seemed disconnected, with her mind willing her muscles to relax. Still, she writhed against the spasms and cold sweats, vaguely aware of someone placing a cool washcloth to her forehead, ice chips to her lips.

The cramping began to subside and Chelsea gradually returned to the real world. Her eyes fluttered open. She felt so weak. She glanced around the small hospital room, spotting Jake slumped in a chair.

He slept in what looked like an incredibly uncomfortable position, still wearing his dirty clothing. The only addition to his attire was a too-small shirt. She guessed someone had lent it to him. His black hair was mussed and his face was still smudged from the incident this morning. How could a two-hundred-pound man look so vulnerable?

He shifted and opened his eyes. Shaking his head as if to clear away some confusion, he straightened and looked at her. When he saw that she was awake, he stood and moved to the side of the bed. The tender, powerful emotion she saw in his eyes was too much to handle in her weakened state. She had to close her eyes against it.

"You awake?" he murmured with a rusty voice.

"Yes," she sighed and opened her eyes again. "Thanks," she said with a wan smile.

Jake turned his head to the side and took a deep, trembling breath. And if Jake had been the kind of man to shed tears, Chelsea would have sworn he was fighting them right then. He touched her hair with fingers that weren't quite so steady. "You scared the hell out of me."

She gave him a look of disbelief. "A little pest like me couldn't scare you, Jake."

He gazed at her intently. "Yeah, well you did. I didn't like it. So, don't ever do it again."

Reaching for his hand, she twined her fingers with his, sensing he needed this connection as much as she. "I'll stay away from black widow spiders, if you'll stay away from falling logs."

He wrapped her hand between both of his own and bent his head closer to hers. And though she felt her eyelids growing heavier, she couldn't prevent her hand from reaching to touch his stubbled cheek. "I owe you," he muttered.

His voice held too much pain. She felt his regret, his guilt. Her lips curved into a smile. With a cheekiness that stole the last of her strength, she said, "I'll take the watch." Then she drifted off to sleep.

She awoke again in the morning to find herself alone. Her tongue felt furry and she suddenly realized she'd had nothing to eat or drink since yesterday morning. After signalling a nurse, both matters were taken care of with a minimum of fuss.

She ate sparingly, still feeling a lingering nausea. Then she took a shower and lay there with the television on. Chelsea let out a bored sigh and idly flicked the ends of her damp hair.

Realizing she had no business remaining in the hospital, she completed a futile search of the room for her clothes. Wrapping an extra hospital nightgown around herself, she walked to the nurse's station. "I want to leave," she said with as much dignity as she could muster. "If you could please locate my clothing, I'd appreciate it."

The middle-aged nurse raised her eyebrows. "The doctor hasn't released you. You'll have to wait until the proper papers are signed."

Chelsea felt confused and a little panicky. Though most of her pain had disappeared, she felt just enough out of sorts to want to get away from there and into her own bed. "Could you call him, please?"

The woman shook her head. "Dr. Bates won't be in until this afternoon."

Dr. Bates. She didn't even remember the man. "Well, couldn't someone else sign my release papers?" Chelsea glanced around, spotting a balding man bearing a stethoscope. "Doctor," she called to him as he strode past the nurse's station. "Doctor, I'm not sick anymore. I'd like to go home."

The elderly man fixed her with a frowning gaze that turned to amusement. His eyes sparkled behind his wire-rimmed bifocals. "Well, we certainly wouldn't want to get a reputation for keeping healthy people in the hospital, would we?"

The kindly doctor teased her into her first smile of the morning. After examining her and declaring her fit, he signed her release papers. By lunchtime Chelsea was walking out of the hospital wearing a borrowed uniform.

She briefly considered calling Jake and asking him for a ride, but dismissed it when she remembered he'd missed the entire day at work yesterday and would probably be extremely busy.

So she did what any well-bred southern woman would do in her circumstance. She called a cab.

The fee was exorbitant. But she brushed off her concern over the expense, when she reached the guest house and breathed a sigh of relief.

She stripped off the borrowed dress and pulled on the T-shirt Jake had lent her. To her dismay, her minor exertions had weakened her. So she crawled into bed and promptly fell asleep.

A short time later, a stomping noise awakened her. A feeling of unease swept over her. Tension stiffened her body. She sat up and pushed her hair from her face. When she saw Jake at the doorway, relief coursed through her.

"Hi," she said, her voice husky from sleep. She self-consciously pulled the covers more firmly around her. Patting ineffectually at her hair, she grimaced at how she must look.

With his face set in a scowl, he stood there holding sacks of what smelled like hamburgers. "What the hell are you doing here?"

Chelsea propped up her pillows and leaned back against them. "Well, I was trying to get some sleep. However," she said with a smile, "if you've brought my lunch, then I guess I'll be eating."

If possible, his scowl grew deeper. "You were half out of your mind with pain yesterday. You've got no business being out of the hospital. I oughta haul you back there right now. How'd you get home anyway?"

Chelsea chose to ignore his statements about where

he thought she should be and answered his question. "I called a cab."

"A cab." He looked horrified. "Why didn't you call me?"

Shrugging, she replied, "I assumed you'd be too busy after missing work yesterday. I didn't want to bother you." She sighed, feeling awkward about trying to explain herself. "So what's in the bags?" she asked, changing the subject.

Jake glanced down as if he'd just remembered holding them. "Lunch. I thought you might want something to eat besides hospital food. I'll bring you a tray."

Forgetting about her state of undress, she pushed off the covers and swung her feet to the floor. "Oh, no. I don't have to eat in bed."

She started to stand, but the look in Jake's eyes stopped her abruptly.

His gaze encompassed her from the top of her disheveled head to her coral-tinted toenails in what could only be described as pure masculine approval. She flushed under his lingering appraisal.

The heat in his black eyes as he studied her bare legs was enough to make her toes curl into the carpet. "Jake?" she said weakly.

His head snapped up, but his eyes remained smoky with arousal. He cleared his throat. "You stay where you are. I'll bring a tray."

Chelsea collapsed weakly on the bed covering herself with the bedspread. Lord help her, she was susceptible to this man. She felt herself sliding closer to the edge of an emotional pit with each passing day. But she clung furiously to her restraint because she knew with an odd certainty that although Jake might be attracted to her, he wasn't a forever kind of man.

Hearing his returning footsteps, she pasted a smile on her face. He placed the tray across her lap and sat down on the edge of the bed, waiting expectantly.

The sight of him on her bed set off a heady train of thoughts completely unrelated to food. She sat in silence while her roving mind considered the sensual possibilities. His pale-blue pullover contrasted attractively with his dark complexion. Chelsea was mesmerized by the sprinkling of dark hair revealed at the open collar of his shirt.

When he raised a dark eyebrow, she found herself clearing her own throat. Her cheeks heated and she forced her attention to the food before her. "This was very kind of you. Not necessary, but I appreciate it. Let's see. A cheeseburger with everything, french fries, and catsup." She eyed the drink container and her lips stretched into a smile.

"It's a strawberry milkshake. You said strawberry's your favorite," he pointed out.

Chelsea took a deep breath and averted her eyes. Her heart caught. Such a small thing.

She felt herself sliding.

Most people would find it silly, the fact that Jake had remembered her preference for strawberry.

She slid a little further.

But it meant very much to her. It meant he was paying more attention to her than she'd thought.

Chelsea looked up to thank him and saw an

expression of hope, a look that said he wanted to please her in some small way.

And Chelsea fell right over the edge.

"Are you going to eat?"

She was in love with Jake. Chelsea kept the turmoil she felt hidden inside and wondered how she was going to eat anything ever again. "Uh, yes," she murmured, and ate a tiny bite of the burger. Though she chewed it thoroughly, it still felt like she was trying to swallow a rock.

Her throat was dry, her palms clammy. What on earth was she going to do? She was in love with Jake. And he wanted her out of White Bluff and his life altogether.

She nibbled sparingly on a french fry.

"Chelsea, are you sick again?" Jake lifted her chin with a long finger. She shivered.

He frowned. "Have you got a fever?" Then he put his hand against her forehead. His touch singed her.

Yes, she thought, but not the kind you're talking about. Out of self-preservation, she leaned away from him. "I guess my appetite's not quite back, yet. The doctor told me the symptoms might continue for a while longer."

He scowled. "I knew you shouldn't have left the hospital."

Wanting to remove that possibility from his mind, she gave a light laugh. "I know why you want me in the hospital," she mocked. "That way, I won't be getting in your way at the office or intruding on your life of seclusion out here."

His expression grew pained and he looked as if he was about to protest when she continued. "I don't need a hospital. I don't need food, right now." She handed him the tray. "I need a nap," she said firmly.

Reluctantly, he took the tray and stood. "You have to eat sometime. I'll bring you something tonight. What—"

"That's not necessary."

In a tone that brooked no argument, he said, "You will eat something tonight if I have to feed you with my own hands. Tell me what you want."

Chelsea refused to look at his hands after that last statement and requested the first food that came to mind. "Soup and sandwich."

"You've got it." He hesitated then stepped closer to the bed, stunning her by planting a gentle kiss on her head. "Sweet dreams, babe."

He turned and left the room. And Chelsea thought she'd exercised a great deal of control by waiting until he closed the door before letting out an audible groan.

That day marked a turning point in their relationship. She didn't know if the change occurred because she'd realized she was in love with him, or if it was due to the fact that Jake became more attentive and open. To her mind, it didn't really matter why the change. She was just going to enjoy his attention as long as it lasted. Although she doubted it would last forever.

He brought her simple dinners the next two evenings. Then, as Chelsea began to feel better, she fixed supper for the both of them. If nothing else, she concluded wryly, he found her cooking irresistible. Those were crumbs, she thought, when she wanted Jake to find her irresistible.

They argued about her returning to work.

"You're not ready. What if you have a relapse?" he said as he finished up a brownie on Friday evening.

"I'm tired of staying home. I'm bored." When he started to interrupt, she held up a hand. "We've discussed this before, Jake. You're not my keeper."

"Well, you need one," he said darkly.

She couldn't resist teasing him when he wore that disgruntled expression on his face. "Are you applying for the position?"

His eyes narrowed and raked her body. "Don't tempt me."

Her heart gave a little jump because that's exactly what she wanted to do.

They finally compromised on her working half-days for the next week. Chelsea neglected to tell him she would be very busy at night for the next ten days. She had to get her dance classes ready for their upcoming performance.

On Saturday morning, she left for the community center and posted extra rehearsal times for her students. She ran into Anita on her way out the door.

"I've got to pick up some papers to grade. Have lunch with me and give me the scoop on your spider bite. I didn't get to talk to you very long on the phone the other day." Anita passed by in a blur before she could answer.

Chelsea chuckled. "I'd love to," she called after Anita.

Later, when the two women shared an enjoyable hour at a local taco stand, Chelsea related her accident to the accompaniment of Anita's shudders and grimaces. She asked what kind of dance would probably go over best at the local business owners' meeting. Anita gave her some helpful ideas. They parted with a promise to get together again soon.

On Monday, she arrived at work after lunch. Al put an arm around her in a paternal hug. "You had us worried. Are you sure you should be here? You look fine, but I don't know. We don't want you rushing things."

His concern warmed her. She wasn't accustomed to such genuine affection even from her mother. Chelsea squeezed him lightly in return. "Thank you. But I'm fine." She grimaced. "I think I'd be more likely to die from boredom than the spider bite."

Al guffawed and went back to the warehouse. A little later, Jerry walked in. His face lit up when he saw her. "Miss Collins, are you feeling okay? Everybody around here was all upset when we heard about your accident."

"Al told me. It was nice of y'all to be so concerned about me. I'm fine. And I appreciate the card you sent me last week. It was very kind of you, Jerry."

The boy's face flushed a dusky red. "Aw, it wasn't nothing. I wish I could have done more."

"Thank you." She paused and voiced what was in the back of her mind. "Jerry, my dance class is performing two numbers for a business meeting next week. We'd like to do one song with a Mexican flavor. Do you know any musicians and singers who might be willing to help us out on short notice?''

He hesitated. "Well, my brother sings with a bunch of his friends. If it means they get to stand up and be noticed in front of a big crowd, then they'd probably do it."

Chelsea felt wary. She wasn't in a position to be able to be choosy, but Jerry's brother hadn't struck her as a very dependable sort. "I need someone I can count on. I know he's your brother, but do you think he'd cut out at the last minute?"

"I won't lie to you, Miss Collins. Steve can be a real jerk, but if he says he's going to be somewhere, then he always shows up. That's why my mom asks him to pick me up after work."

She thought it over a minute longer. Then she shrugged. She didn't have any other alternatives. She wrote down the number for the community center. "Please tell Steve if he thinks he can do it to leave a message at the community center and come tomorrow night around five."

Jerry nodded and folded the paper into his pocket.

Later, at closing time, Chelsea opened the door to Jake's office and waved good-night to him. He was in the midst of a discussion with a supplier, so he waved back. She sighed as she made her way to her car. A part of her was excited by the anticipated performance. But she was going to miss sharing the evening meal with Jake.

Chelsea heard footsteps behind her and turned. It was Jake. Her pulse picked up.

"You're going home, aren't you?" he asked.

"No. I'll be at the community center every night this week. My classes will be giving a little performance for a luncheon next week."

"Every night?" He didn't look pleased

"Yes, every night," she said firmly. "There's some leftover beef stew in my refrigerator if you want it." She lifted her shoulders. "Feel free to eat. I won't be home until seven tonight."

"Are you sure you should be—"

Chelsea cut him off, knowing his argument was useless. "I'm fine. Besides, this is a wonderful opportunity to bring in some more donations to the community center."

"Don't push yourself."

"I won't." Chelsea opened her car door. She turned and found him directly in front of her. His eyes were so warm. Later, she would wonder what had possessed her to be so bold, but she didn't stop to think. On impulse, she stretched and brushed a quick, light kiss on his hard mouth.

She saw the surprise and pleasure in his eyes. Her nerve deserted her. "See ya later," she said huskily and got into the car.

Jake watched her leave in bemusement. His lips still burned from her gentle touch. He just wished it hadn't been so quick. When he thought of kissing Chelsea, and he thought of it often, he envisioned endless passionate kisses and bringing her feminine body to life under his hands.

Her car went out of sight. He turned back to the office with a lighter step. Whistling, he planned the evening ahead. He could wait until seven o'clock to eat dinner. He'd gotten used to sharing dinner with her and found he liked it. He liked it enough not to want to go back to the old way of eating beans out of a can to the sound of a Wolfgang Amadeus Mozart's concerto or sonata.

It's just that she's a great cook, he assured himself. But he knew he was lying.

That evening, Chelsea pulled up to the guest house, surprised to find her light on. She was even more surprised when she smelled hot beefstew and found Jake in the kitchen.

Freshly showered with his hair damp, he wore worn denim jeans that proclaimed his masculinity and a T-shirt that revealed his impressive shoulders and muscles. He grinned. "The rolls and the beefstew are ready. Do you want iced tea?"

Still dazed by his presence, she nodded. "Yes. But what are you doing here? I thought you'd eat earlier."

He shrugged. "I got busy and forgot about the time. So I figured I'd just wait." He looked up from pouring the tea. "Do you mind?"

"No!" she said loudly, then lowered her voice. "No. I'm just surprised."

His hard mouth stretched into a very male grin. "Good." She'd never seen him smile this much. Her heart thumped wildly.

Feeling befuddled, she dropped her carryall in the den and eased onto a bar stool. He set her at ease with questions about her plans for her ballet classes. The simple meal passed companionably.

He seemed in such a good mood that Chelsea decided to broach a subject that had been disturbing her. "Jake," she said while she cleaned the bar, "we've talked about this before, but could you tell me when my father gave you the gold watch?"

His face closed up immediately and she almost regretted bringing up the sticky issue. But she wanted to know more about the circumstances surrounding the gift.

"I didn't take it from him. He gave it to me three months before he died."

Puzzled, she furrowed her brow. "But why three months before he died? That doesn't make sense." If anything, Jake seemed to close up more after her innocent questions.

"Jake," she implored him. "I'm not accusing you. You seem to forget what little contact I had with my father the last few years." Chelsea lightly touched his taut arm. "I know that watch was important to him. Is it asking too much for you to tell me about him?"

Jake gave a heavy sigh. "No. You're not asking too much." He put a guiding hand on her shoulder. "Let's go in the den."

They sat beside each other on the sofa. Waiting in silence, Chelsea watched Jake pull the watch from his pocket. The antique gleamed from the light of the nearby lamp. He held the timepiece as if it were rare and priceless. And Chelsea got her first indication that the watch was as important to him as it was to her.

His attachment to the watch did nothing to appease her own longing for her father's treasure. "May I hold it?" she asked.

He paused, then handed the watch to her. It was warm from his touch. The sensation of holding it in her hands conjured up a hundred memories. "I remember playing with it when I was a little girl. He always warned me to be careful with it. He was never without it." She laughed in remembrance. "He must have told me the story about how my grandmother bought it for my grandfather ten times. I loved hearing it every time."

He leaned back into the sofa and crossed his ankle across his knee. "He told me about that, too." Expelling a heavy breath, Jake pinched the bridge of his nose.

Chelsea felt her heart go out to him. She touched her hand to his. He looked into her eyes and laced their fingers. A lump formed in her throat. She felt oddly bound to him.

"He gave me the watch three months before he died. It was my birthday. Ed didn't give many emotional speeches, even when his time got closer." He squeezed her hand tighter. "He told me how proud he was of me, of my accomplishments, of the man I'd become. Then he said he wanted me to have something that had meant a great deal to him."

Jake swallowed hard. "The watch. I told him I couldn't take it, that it shouldn't belong to me. Then he got this odd smile on his face. And he told me he'd been lucky enough to have a princess for a little girl. He hated being apart from you, but he was always sure of your love. 'You can't ask for much more than that,' he said. 'But I got you, too. If I could've had a son, I would've wanted one just like you. Take the watch, Jake. And have good memories of me.' ''

Jake's jaw worked with emotion. "It was all I could do to say thank you. I've kept it in my pocket ever since." He turned eyes full of turmoil to Chelsea. "Nobody's ever given me anything that meant so much. I have nothing from my mother and father except for a few pictures and their wedding bands."

She blinked back tears. She'd been so foolishly jealous over the watch. Her father had loved her, and she was thankful he'd had enough love to share with Jake. She felt small and petty about her previous suspicions and offers to buy the timepiece.

Taking a deep breath, she said good-bye to the jealousy the watch had evoked. Then she pressed the golden treasure into Jake's hand. She tried to remove her fingers, but he prevented her. He stared into her eyes and carefully braided their fingers together over the watch.

She quivered at the powerful emotion traveling between them. It was more than desire, though there was desire. It was more than grief. If she wasn't so afraid to hope, she'd call it love.

But her opportunity for thinking passed. Jake leaned into her and kissed her. Helplessly, she opened her mouth in invitation to his passionate expression. Their tongues dueled until they settled into a sliding, sensuous rhythm.

A fire coursed through her veins, making her gasp with the force of her own desire. She pressed her sensitive breasts into his strong chest, yearning for the ultimate closeness. A shudder ran through his big body.

Reluctantly, he drew his lips from hers. His eyes reminded her of the sea, tempestuous with desire.

"Don't tell me to move in with Anita. I'm not going to," she said breathlessly.

He placed the watch on the coffee table and turned back to her. "I don't want you to go anywhere," he said in a gruff voice and took her in his arms to kiss her again.

EIGHT

The din of high-pitched voices filled the makeshift dressing room in spite of Chelsea's efforts to calm the performers. She couldn't keep the smile from her face as she straightened a five-year-old's tutu. But then her face had been wearing a perpetual smile for the entire week.

"You're getting silly," she scolded herself and promptly started humming. She'd never experienced a more perfect week in her life. Jake had been attentive, amorous, yet controlled. And she was beginning to hope that he was falling a little bit for her.

Chelsea sighed and returned her attention to her students. She clapped her hands in a fruitless effort to get their attention. Dismissing her mother's disapproving face from her mind, she placed two fingers against her lips and whistled the way her father had taught her.

Instant silence.

She smiled. "It's almost time for you to line up. Now, I don't want you to worry. Just do your best and have a good time. The people out there are very excited that you've come to dance for them."

A helper gave her the signal from the door. "Okay, I need my ballerinas," Chelsea said. After a flurry of motion and the soothing of some ruffled nerves, the dancers moved into the stage area of the city hall auditorium.

Her eyes burned with threatening tears as she watched the students perform the simple dance at their earnest best. The number ended and the girls ran back, their faces glowing with excitement and pride. Chelsea doled out quick hugs right before she lined the other girls up for the second number.

Crossing her fingers that all their practicing would pay off, she led the second group out. She nodded at Steve and his band, who had been more dependable than she could have hoped. And the music began.

Jake sat up a little straighter when the second group of dancers came out. The good-natured tittering swept through the crowd with reason. The performers, who ranged in age from five to twelve, were dressed in Mexican peasant dress. Shy, dark eyes peeked out from beneath straw hats laden with fruit.

When the music started the girls struck a challenging feminine pose; hands on hips and chins lifted with demure smiles. The singer told the hard-luck story of a man visiting a nightspot south of the border. The poor sap had almost been torn limb from limb due to his infatuation with a pretty senorita imploring him to come a little bit closer.

The little girls moved in a naturally graceful rhythm to the Latin beat. Although Jake felt a measure of pride in Chelsea's students success, he still couldn't believe he was here. A luncheon for business owners wasn't his usual activity. But when Chelsea explained how much his presence would mean to her, there was no way he could refuse.

The crowd murmured their delight when Chelsea appeared dressed in her own peasant blouse and skirt. The only aspect of her costume that seemed out of place was the ace bandage wrapped around her ankle. She'd overdone it again. Jake's heart thumped more quickly in his chest at the sight of her. She was so lovely. Who could resist her?

And they didn't. Much to the audience's surprise, Chelsea moved from the stage to invite the mayor to join in the dance. "Well, I'll be damned," he muttered. The mayor didn't even put up a token protest. With a broad smile, he playfully imitated her steps. A few of the older dancers cajoled some other members of the audience into shedding their inhibitions and dancing.

Before Jake knew it, Chelsea was standing before him with her arms outstretched in invitation. He shook his head no, glancing around self-consciously. She'd turned on the radio in the den one evening earlier this week and asked him to dance with her. But he'd felt uncomfortable and refused.

Right now, she held firm. With a determined glint

in her eye, she clasped his hand and gently pulled. Her lips were set in a pout that begged his attention.

"Aw, hell," he said, and gave up the fight.

He moved stiffly, but she felt like heaven in his arms. He tried to think back to when he'd last danced with a woman and couldn't remember. Had it been gym class in junior high school? He hadn't gone to a prom in high school.

"See, this isn't so bad," Chelsea smiled at him.

"Yeah, but having you in my arms makes me want to kiss you in a way that might shock the good citizens of White Bluff."

Color suffused her face becomingly. Her eyes darkened with such sensual awareness he considered dragging her away so they could be alone. Leaning forward on tiptoe, she spoke in a voice that was a caress against his ear, "Hold that thought."

Then she left, and Jake was left only with the soft floral scent of her and the memory of her warmth in his arms. Although he hesitated to admit it, that was his biggest fear. That he would give his heart to Chelsea only to be left with memories of her when she went back east.

Still, he didn't know how much longer he could maintain control over their growing passion. He wanted her so much and she seemed willing.

Returning to his seat, Jake kept his eyes on Chelsea as he lit a cigarette. The music stopped and the audience's applause lasted for an appreciative several minutes. When the room grew quiet, she gave an earnest appeal for support for the community center and the upcoming benefit.

Jake saw several people reaching into their pockets for checkbooks. Chelsea and her students had been a rousing success. Still, in the back of his mind he wondered what would happen next year to the community center, to her ballet students, to him, when Chelsea left White Bluff for greener pastures.

"You're awfully quiet. Is something wrong?" Chelsea took another bite of lemon mousse and studied Jake. He'd uttered about five complete sentences during dinner. His face wore a brooding expression. It worried her.

Jake met her gaze then looked away. "Nah, I've just been thinking."

She removed the dessert dishes from the table and led Jake into the den. "Thinking about what?"

He ran a long calloused finger on the inside of her wrist. She shivered. He noticed her small movement and looked into her eyes with a spark of heat in his own. His other hand traveled to her hair, smoothing and stroking. "Thinking about when you're going to leave."

Chelsea had to fight to concentrate on his words instead of on what his hands were doing to her body. Her eyelids seemed to want to droop and her arms begged to be around his neck. She wrinkled her brow in confusion. "I'm not going anywhere."

"Chelsea, the will only stipulates that you remain active in the business for a year. You'll be free to go then." He said that last statement as if it required a great deal of effort.

She wondered if it was possible that Jake was

afraid of her leaving. Her practical side insisted it was ridiculous. Jake wasn't afraid of anything. But the emotional Chelsea, the one who was in love with Jake, came alive with hope.

She stroked his cheek with gentle fingers, saw both the agony and the fire in his dark eyes. Wetting her lips, she said, "I have other reasons for being here, Jake. There's my involvement with the community center."

Running her finger along his lower lip, she felt him stiffen. "I've made lots of friends. But I have a confession to make. The main reason I want to stay . . ." She leaned forward until her lips were a breath from his, "is you," she whispered.

He let out a groan and took her mouth in a devastating kiss. His tongue searched and plundered her yielding mouth in a way that rocked her senses. She gripped his shoulders when his mouth left a trail of fire down her neck to her collarbone.

In mind-drugging abandon, she sought his mouth again, savoring his rich male taste. When he pushed the peasant blouse from her shoulders and brushed aside the lacy bra from her breasts, there was no thought of protest. He cupped her breasts gently in his big hands, his thumbs drawing increasingly smaller circles until he caressed the hard tips.

A burst of pleasure surged through her. "Oh," she gasped.

He stopped. "Did I hurt you?"

"No," she pressed against him. Her words came out disjointedly. "It just . . . feels . . . so good."

He lowered his head, dropping light kisses on her

heavy mounds. Then he took her nipple into his mouth, sucking and laving it with his tongue. The fire was burning her. She buried her fingers into his crisp dark hair and kissed his head.

Raising his head, he drew her hand to his chest. She felt his heart thump wildly. "See what you do to me." He put her fingers to his shirt buttons. "I want to feel you against me."

His rough request made her mouth dry and her fingers stumbled in their effort to do his bidding. When she finally succeeded in releasing the buttons, she boldly pushed it from his shoulders. She ran adoring fingers over his well-defined muscles and twirled her polished nails among the mat of hair on his chest.

He groaned at her ministrations, pulled her to him, only to sigh when he felt the pressure of her breasts against his chest. They kissed longingly for what could have been minutes or hours. Chelsea had no concept of time. Her only reality was Jake and the sensations he aroused within her.

Sweeping her into his arms, he stood and strode into the darkened bedroom. "I want you, Chelsea. Tell me you feel the same way."

She felt his need and knew what he was asking. She couldn't deny him. "I love you, Jake."

His mouth clamped down on hers, allowing neither words nor thoughts. Without releasing her lips, he followed her down on the bed. His hands slid under her skirt, caressing her soft thighs. A dull ache began to throb in the center of her being. She moaned into his mouth.

He pulled away slightly and Chelsea felt a sliver of feminine apprehension at his savage expression. His nostrils flared with labored breaths, his mouth was set in a strained line. When he removed her skirt and tugged on her panties, she sought his reassurance. "Jake," she said breathlessly. "I love you."

"Are you protected?" he asked, nuzzling her neck and massaging her hips with big, tender hands.

It took a moment for the question to penetrate. Birth control. "Yes," she murmured hazily, "I'm on the pill."

"Good."

Then, in a matter of seconds, her panties joined his clothes on the floor. And he was touching all her secret places, driving every thought but Jake from her mind.

She kissed his strong neck and nipped at his full lower lip. She caressed his chest and abdomen, then went lower still with curious fingers. Her seductive movements, born of instinct, broke Jake's tenuous control.

"Oh, baby," he groaned. "I can't wait for you any longer."

She arched against him, seeking release from the ever-tightening tension. Jake coaxed her thighs apart. He kissed her lips and thrust into her at the same moment.

His mouth caught her gasp of shock, and he felt her slight jerk at the invasion.

Staring in surprise, Jake pulled back slightly, holding himself perfectly still. "You're a virgin."

Chelsea winced as her untried body continued to

accommodate his fullness. She gave a half-smile. "Not anymore."

With Chelsea's warm, fluid body sheathing him so tightly, he was on the verge of exploding. But his emotions were in an uproar. He hadn't known she was innocent, and he was appalled that he'd hurt her.

"Why didn't you tell me?" he whispered, running a soothing hand over her cheek.

Her whole body turned pink. "I guess you made me forget."

At her sexy little confession, Jake swelled painfully and knew they would have to stop or he would end up hurting her more. He began to pull away, but Chelsea wrapped her legs around his back, trapping him in her tempting femininity.

Jake stared at the irresistible sight before him. Chelsea with her hair tousled, blue eyes heavy with passion, lips red and wet from his kisses. Her breasts were swollen and flushed, the nipples, hard little beads of sensation.

"Don't stop," she pleaded. Chelsea arched again.

Jake groaned and was lost.

Several minutes passed after his final thrust and Chelsea knew she'd missed something from this most intimate encounter. Her lower body buzzed with a stretched, burning sensation.

Still, she had Jake in her arms, and the knowledge that she had brought his pleasure pleased her. At this moment, she was closer to him than she'd ever been to anyone before. She felt his breathing settle into a relaxed pattern.

Pulling his head from her cheek, he opened his mouth to speak.

Chelsea shook her head and placed a finger on his lips. "Don't talk," she said, staring into his eyes. "Just hold me."

So he cuddled her close and held her for a while. He sensed her underlying restlessness, however, and began to touch her first with long, soothing strokes that relaxed her enough to allow him to please her. He rubbed her back and tickled her neck. He pleasured her breasts with mouth and hands until her skin grew warm and her movements seeking.

The heat turned to sensual fever when he murmured dark words of praise in her ear as he stroked her feminine core. Her eyes grew glazed and she clung to him. Her body jerked and his mouth caught her gasp again, but this time her response was born of pleasure not pain. He watched, losing a little of himself, as she came apart in his arms, calling his name. The thought came to him that he'd like to hole up in this room with Chelsea and throw away the key. And that scared the hell out of him.

Chelsea slept while Jake stared at the ceiling.

In the middle of the night, Chelsea awoke. She felt a chill where there'd once been warmth. She glanced at the luminous dial of her alarm clock, two a.m. Then her gaze found Jake seated on the side of her bed with his head in his hands. He was wearing his jeans.

A strange foreboding grabbed at her. She wet her suddenly dry lips. "Jake," she began and then stopped because she couldn't think of anything else to say.

He turned and sighed. "You're awake."

She nodded.

"I'm sorry. I didn't mean to wake you." Standing, he rubbed the back of his neck. "I'm sorry about everything. I had no idea you were . . . inexperienced."

Chelsea smiled and felt a bit of relief. He was just uncomfortable with how he'd found out. She sat up. "It's okay, Jake," she reassured him. "I told you, I love you."

"You don't mean that. You're just saying that because I'm your first. Lots of women get confused about their first experience with sex."

She felt a sinking sensation in the pit of her stomach. "Sex. It was more than that, Jake, and you know it. I told you I love you and I meant it. Why else would I be in this bed with you?"

Jake shook his head. "Sweetheart, people hit the sack for lots of reasons. Most of them have nothing to do with love and a lot to do with lust." He pinned her with his gaze. "Did you really think this was about love? Love and marriage aren't in my present or future."

Chelsea sat there, stunned, staring at him, unable to compose her thoughts.

With an unsteady hand, Jake pulled the sheet up over her revealed breast, then looked away as if he couldn't bear the sight of her.

"Just try to forget about this . . ." His voice trailed off. He must have known the statement was ridiculous. Jake looked at her one last time, his face a picture of self-contempt. "I'm sorry. I've gotta go."

Her heart leapt into her throat. "Wait!" she called. But he continued as if she hadn't spoken, his only response the slam of her front door.

Chelsea just stared in confusion. He'd acted as if he'd wanted her more than anything. He'd been so gentle, yet passionate. She'd been so sure of his love.

The realization of his feelings came to her slowly, insidiously creeping from her mind to her heart and stomach. He hadn't loved her. He'd only wanted to use her. Sickened by his betrayal, she sat there on the bed where he had been her first lover.

She felt a hysterical urge to cry but tamped it down. She fought an equally strong urge to go over to his house and murder him. Shaking her head at her confused thoughts, she stood.

She had to get out of here. The picture of his face contorted with contempt kept flashing in her mind. Her humiliation burned her skin. The fact that she was still undressed made it even worse.

She reached blindly into her closet, pulling on the first thing she found, a yellow shirtwaist dress. Her fingers trembled as she buttoned it and she tried not to think of how her fingers had trembled on Jake's buttons.

Grabbing a suitcase, she flung it open. She jerked open her drawers and threw an unknown assortment of clothing into the suitcase. Cosmetics, she thought, and grabbed her makeup bag from the bathroom. Her anguish increased tenfold when she caught sight of her reflection in the mirror. Bruised lips, pale cheeks, overbright eyes, wild hair.

She closed her eyes and viciously brushed her hair, securing it into a ponytail. The cool water she splashed on her face soothed her. She walked back into the bedroom, snapped the suitcase shut, and headed for her front door.

When she caught sight of his discarded shirt rumpled on the sofa next to her peasant blouse, she had to fight the urge not to sob. Instead, she took both garments out the door with her and threw them into the trash can outside.

After locking the door behind her, Chelsea took one last lingering look at the deceptively quiet night. The stars twinkled and the breeze rustled the hem of her dress. Mozart came and nuzzled against her.

How could everything appear so normal when she was falling apart? She patted the dog, whispered an endearment to him, then got into her car.

She started the engine and without looking back disappeared into the night.

After driving for hours, she pulled into a luxury hotel in Tucson near dawn. Chelsea fell into bed and didn't wake until noon. She groaned, shielding her eyes against the sun filtering through the window. Her head felt as if it was the target for a wrecking ball.

She rummaged for her cosmetic case, praying she'd packed aspirin. Sending up a murmur of thanks when she located it, she took the medication with water from the bathroom.

A grimace crossed her face at the sight of her face in the mirror. She looked like she felt; emotionally ravaged. She felt the burn of threatening tears behind her eyes and pressed her fingers tightly against them to staunch the flow.

She would not cry. Not today. The pain was too close, the wound too recent. She squared her shoulders and flipped on the shower. The water washed away Jake's lingering scent, leaving her with an odd feeling of relief and loss.

She knew she couldn't stay in the room moping all day long. So, once again, she fell back on her upbringing.

She went shopping.

"Where is she?" Jake muttered for the thousandth time. He'd felt uneasy when he'd gotten up on Sunday morning to find her car gone. The feeling had grown to apprehension and anger by Monday morning. And now that it was Tuesday, he was just plain sweating it out.

He checked his watch, wondering how time could pass so slowly. After briefly considering calling her mother, Jake dismissed that notion and contacted Anita. But Anita hadn't known any more than he did.

Had she really gone back to Richmond? When he thought of the lost expression on her face Saturday night, he cringed. How could he have been so callous about Ed Collins's daughter? She was so beautiful and alluring he'd just assumed she was also experienced.

To find out she was innocent had been too much. He didn't want to think about why she was still so important to him.

But the sad truth of the matter was that every time Jake thought about Chelsea leaving White Bluff and never returning, he broke out in a cold sweat.

He ground his cigarette into the ashtray full of butts and glanced down at the invoice he'd been going over for the last hour. When Jake discovered she'd gone ahead and ordered the signs he'd rejected, he'd been so angry that he cancelled the order. Of course, that was yesterday.

Today, he'd consider setting out perfume samples if it meant she'd come back. Jake grunted in disgust at himself. He stood, tossed a pencil on the desk, and stared out the window.

There was a knock at his office door.

"Yes," he said, still distracted by his thoughts.

Al walked in with a wary expression on his face. Jake acknowledged him with a nod, realizing he'd bitten just about every one of his employees' heads off in the past two days. It was a wonder they didn't all go on strike.

"Anita called just a minute ago. Chelsea called her." Al removed his hat. "She's back in town, but—"

Jake didn't let him finish. He grabbed his car keys and made for the door. "Thanks, Al. Close up for me, will you?"

Then he strode out of the office, too intent on getting home to notice Al's voice calling after him.

Twenty minutes later, Jake brought the jeep to a

jolting stop and hopped out. He knocked on the guest house door but didn't wait for her to answer. He strode past the kitchen and den right into her bedroom.

Chelsea looked up at him in surprise. Her cheeks colored and she looked away, returning to her task of packing. Piles of clothing lay on the bed, ready to be placed in the suitcases and boxes.

A knot formed in Jake's stomach. "Where have you been?"

"Away."

That irritated him. "You running back to Richmond?"

Her back stiffened and she glared at him over her shoulder. "No." Then she turned back to the clothes. "I'm just following your advice and moving in with Anita."

He relaxed slightly. At least she wasn't leaving White Bluff. Although he wasn't nearly as happy as he should be about her moving in with Anita, he would still see her at work.

"And I've decided to work an earlier schedule. I think I'd be more . . . comfortable working the same hours the other men do."

His heart sank again. Chelsea was tactfully informing him that she was rearranging her work schedule to avoid him. She knew he spent most of his morning hours at the work sites. Jake faced the fact that he wanted Chelsea to stay in the guest house and keep working at the office because he wanted to see her every day even if she was mad at him. The only place he wanted her more was in his own house.

He cursed under his breath. If she knew what he was thinking, she'd hit the roof. He'd made a fine mess of things this time.

But she hadn't left yet. Perhaps if he could delay her, she wouldn't leave at all. He said the first thing that came to mind. "That's gonna make things tough for Mozart."

She paused and turned. "Mozart?" She frowned quizzically.

"Yeah, I was hoping you wouldn't mind looking after him when I drive into Phoenix for a state contractor's meeting next week." He'd had no intention of going to the meeting until now.

"Why can't you put him in a kennel?"

Jake shook his head. "Mozart doesn't belong in a kennel. You know what kind of dog he is. He's used to roaming wherever he wants."

Sinking down on the bed, she contemplated his words. Her silky hair fell across her cheek like a curtain as she avidly studied the design of the bedspread. "I guess I could put off moving in with Anita for another week," she said reluctantly.

Jake barely contained his shout of triumph.

Then she stood and faced him squarely. "As long as you agree to meet a few conditions."

Wary, he asked, "Like what?"

"We both know why I want to move into town with Anita." When her face colored, he cursed himself a thousand times.

"If I stay here, I want you to leave me alone," she said with uncharacteristic bluntness. "I won't fix your supper. I won't invite you in for a drink. And

I don't want any more threats or . . ." She looked away, and if anything her face grew more pink. "Seductions," she finished.

He could argue with that last one. In his opinion, Chelsea Collins was seduction incarnate, with her innocent allure. But he'd gotten what he wanted, so he wouldn't quibble over her foolish conditions. At least, not today.

"I agree," he said mildly.

Folding her hands, she gazed up at him. "Fine, I'm glad we understand each other. I'll leave a report on your desk everyday."

He rubbed his chin thoughtfully. "Okay. But you know Jerry's been asking about you. Something about a school project."

A light of remembrance swept over her face and she grimaced. "That's right. I promised to help him with his art project." She sighed. "I have a meeting with the director of the community center tomorrow afternoon. I guess I could meet him after that, if I had a key."

Jake didn't hesitate. He reached into his pocket, removed the key from the ring and held it out to her.

She appeared surprised, but she reached for it.

Jake watched her carefully when he allowed his hand to touch hers a moment longer than necessary.

When she jerked her hand away and nervously fluttered the other one over her hair, he used all his willpower not to reach for her. There were things that needed to be said, but Jake had no idea how to say them.

He just thanked God that she wasn't immune to

him. He gave a brief nod and swaggered out of the room.

Chelsea weakly sank down onto the bed, taking deep calming breaths. She'd hoped to avoid seeing him until she'd gained more control over her emotions. After she'd finished her shopping binge in Tucson, she'd spent a couple of hours crying.

Briefly, she'd considered moving back to Richmond. But that smacked of defeat. So she decided to stay in White Bluff and avoid Jake. Thus far, she'd enjoyed White Bluff and her job. Jake was the only thorn in her side. Why should she let a man dictate where she would live?

But she still felt something for him. Her blood had raced through her veins when he'd walked into her house. And when he touched her. "Oh," she moaned, remembering the tingling feeling in her hand.

But he doesn't love you, she reminded herself. She felt the same ache she always did at the realization. Avoidance, that was the key. It shouldn't be difficult to avoid him if she worked an earlier schedule and taught some extra classes at the community center. The only problem was that she'd given her students a week off after the performance for the Chamber of Commerce. Still, that wouldn't prevent her from practicing. She'd just have to be careful not to overdo.

"I will get over him. I will get over him," she chanted over and over as she put away the clothing.

Four days later, as she entered the office, Chelsea was feeling successful in her campaign to avoid Jake.

The community center provided a welcome respite in the afternoons and evenings when she danced. Her ankle wasn't telling on her, thank goodness.

She'd even made a date with Chris Preston. She found as long as she kept very busy that thoughts of Jake invaded her mind less often. Her vivid dreams told a different story. But she wouldn't focus on that, she told herself. This was going to take time.

Making her way to Jake's office through the darkened building, Chelsea smiled at how cleverly she'd arranged the timing of this meeting with Jerry. She knew Jake often played softball games on Friday nights, so she'd allowed fifteen minutes past closing time.

Hearing two voices in the closed office, she frowned. One was Jerry's. The other was deeper, more mature, the only voice that held the power to raise goosebumps on her flesh. Steeling herself against the onslaught of emotion she always felt in his presence, Chelsea pushed open the door.

He looked wonderful. From his attractively tousled dark hair, to the navy pullover that accentuated his broad form, he filled her eyes with what had become her definition of the perfect man. She gave an inward groan. By all rights, he should look ugly and dirty after a day's work, she wailed to herself.

Their eyes caught and held. Hers distrustful blue, his a hungry brown. At least, that's what she'd have sworn she saw in his eyes as his gaze swept over her. But the moment passed so quickly she must have been mistaken.

"Chelsea, Jerry's been telling me about his school

project. It sounds like you two have been working hard,'' Jake said.

She smiled at Jerry and decided to focus the discussion on him. "The credit goes to Jerry. I only gave him a few books and some suggestions as to how to arrange his report. He wanted me to check it over for him one last time, tonight.'' She hesitated. ''But we don't want to disturb you. Perhaps we should go somewhere else.''

"Oh, no,'' Jake insisted with an innocent grin. ''I'm just doing the books. When Jerry told me you two were planning on working on his project, I went ahead and brought an extra chair in here so you two would be comfortable.''

His words registered, along with the fact that the empty chair was placed right beside Jake's. She took a fortifying breath and sat down. "I see,'' she said slowly, searching his face for hidden motives. When she didn't find any, she gave a shaky smile. "Thank you.''

Clearing her throat, she turned her attention back to Jerry. "Okay, let's see what you've got.''

The boy handed her the folder of paper with a great deal of pride glowing on his face. After five minutes of silence, Chelsea found herself shifting in her chair. She'd reread the last sentence about twenty times and was beginning to think she'd have better luck giving the paper her undivided attention if she was sitting in a circus.

Refusing to look at Jake, she felt rather than saw his gaze on her. She wished she'd chosen to wear something else today. The lilac colored cotton-knit dress skimmed her curves and revealed a generous amount of her bare legs. She'd bought it in Tucson because it was both pretty and cool.

Jake moved his hand and she caught a glimpse of his forearm sprinkled with dark hair in her peripheral vision. The image of his strong arms wrapped around her bare upper body sprang to mind and she practically shuddered at the vivid memory.

She forced her attention back to the paper only to hear the drumming of Jake's fingers on the desk. Struggling through a few more lines, she grew frustrated and turned to ask him to stop.

She opened her mouth, but he spoke first.

"Nice dress," he said his eyes taking a tour of all the secrets the dress hid.

Her cheeks heated at the direction of her thoughts. He seemed to understand because his mouth stretched into a very male grin.

"Thank you," she choked out. He was enjoying her discomfort entirely too much. She'd like to throw something at him. She'd like to erase the smile from the lips that had brought her body to life.

She had to get out of here. She was suffocating in his nearness.

Jerry interrupted her thoughts. "What do you think, Miss Collins?" he asked uncertainly. "Do you think it's okay?"

Taking a deep breath, she reassured him, "It's wonderful. I have just a few more pages. Honestly, you've done such a good job, I don't think I can recommend any changes. And your illustrations are great. I've always admired people who can draw."

Jerry beamed under the praise. "Gosh, thanks. But Jake helped me with the drawings. He showed me how to copy the pictures from the book you gave me."

Surprised, she looked back at Jake. "I didn't know you had artistic talent."

He moved slightly as if uncomfortable with the subject. Then he shrugged and looked at her thoughtfully. "Things aren't always what they seem. We found that out about each other in the beginning."

So true, she thought and felt confused. She looked away unable to meet his probing eyes.

With a tenacity she hadn't known she possessed, Chelsea blocked out everything but Jerry's paper for the next five minutes and finished it. She gave the project the attention it deserved and commended Jerry for his efforts. "If you correct those minor spelling errors I marked, I'm sure you'll get an A." With a feeling of tremendous relief, she stood. "Listen, why don't we celebrate by getting some ice cream? You deserve a reward. I'll give you a ride home and we can stop and get it then."

"You don't have to do that, Miss Collins," Jerry said. But she could tell he would enjoy the small treat.

"I want to. Come on, you've earned it," she insisted, moving to the door.

"I could take you," Jake said as he stood.

Chelsea felt a moment of panic. He wasn't making it easy for her to avoid him. Then she caught sight of the papers on his desk. "Oh, we couldn't do that, Jake," she said sweetly. "After all, you stayed late just so you could finish your paperwork. It's kind of you to offer, but we won't impose.''

He looked as if he was about to protest, then gave a sigh of frustration. He ran his fingers through his hair and impatiently tapped a pencil against the desk. You win this time, his expression said. ''You're right. But I won't always have this paperwork.'' He paused, his eyes daring her and promised, ''Next time.''

''Good night,'' Jerry and Chelsea called as they left the office.

Chelsea wondered why she felt they were engaged in some kind of duel. After all, he'd agreed to her request that they avoid each other. Now he seemed to be challenging her and changing the rules.

So who had been the winner in this latest skirmish? She thought of the memories his gaze had stirred within her.

Still, she had been able to prevent his presence on her outing with Jerry, she assured herself.

His male grin was stamped on her brain.

She decided to call it a draw.

NINE

Confused. Chelsea knitted her brows as she drove home from the community center. Yes, she was definitely confused by Jake's behavior. Prior to this week, he'd borrowed not even so much as a grain of salt from her. But in the last few days, he'd shown up at her door asking for everything from ketchup to sugar and eggs. After the eggs incident, she'd cut the grocery advertisement section from the paper and given it to him as a reminder that White Bluff did indeed possess a few well-stocked grocery stores.

Chelsea stretched her lips into a faint smile. Last night he hadn't come back.

It also seemed that he'd come to the office in the morning more often than usual. She shook her head at the notion. No, she told herself. Jake had wanted her out of his hair since she'd arrived in White Bluff. Any delusions she held that he was trying to be near her were just that. Delusions.

She wouldn't think about him anymore. She'd just finished teaching her dance lessons for the night and she was starving. Pulling the car to a stop, she planned her evening meal. It would have to be something fast; probably a ham sandwich. She'd prefer a steak, but speed was a higher priority at present.

Making her way to the door of the guest house, she caught the scent of an outdoor barbecue. Her mouth watered. Then she heard Jake call out to her.

"Chelsea, c'mon over. I picked up a letter from Richmond for you at the post office box today."

Distracted from her hunger, she raised her eyebrows in astonishment. It was probably from her mother. What on earth would Vivien want now? "Thanks," she said and hurried to where he stood beside the grill.

"It's a little late for dinner, isn't it?" she asked, eyeing the juicy beef ribs.

He gave her a teasing grin. "I took your subtle hint on investigating the grocery store and picked these up on the way home. They look great, don't they?"

"Delicious," she said, feeling her stomach growl at the same time. She blinked in dismay, hoping he hadn't heard.

But he had. His grin grew broader. "I owe you a few meals. I've got enough here for two. Why don't you join me?"

Chelsea hesitated, remembering their agreement not to share meals.

He must have read her mind. "If I remember correctly, you said you wouldn't be fixing meals for me. We didn't say anything about me fixing a meal for you.''

He had a point. Flimsy, her conscience chided. But her stomach won. She muttered something to herself about the spirit being willing, but the flesh weak. ''All right, I accept, but only if you let me contribute something to the meal.''

''More conditions?'' He raised a dark eyebrow.

Her pulse picked up at the gleam in his eye. She ignored his question and continued. ''I have some potato salad and a couple of slices of cheesecake. I'll just go get them, and some tea—''

He stopped her with a strong hand on her arm. She felt the tingle from his touch race through her and looked up at him in surprise. After holding her gaze for a long moment, he seemed to remember why he'd stopped her. Reluctantly, he dropped his hand. ''The letter,'' he murmured and pulled it from his pocket. ''I thought you might want to read it.''

She checked the return address. It was from Vivien. She'd been right. ''Um, I'll be back in a few minutes.''

''The ribs will be ready in about five minutes.''

Nodding absently, she walked away, oddly reluctant to open the letter.

She returned in a more subdued mood, her mind still on the letter from Vivien. After setting the paper plates on the picnic table along with the food she'd brought, she heard Jake speak her name with a hint of exasperation.

''Chelsea, didn't you hear me?''

''Oh, I'm sorry. What were you saying?''

"Was the letter important?" He flipped the ribs onto a platter.

Fussing with the flatware, she shrugged. "Not really. It's the same old thing. My mother finds it difficult to understand why I would choose to work for a construction company and live in a guest house in what she calls a second-rate town in the hottest state of the union." She stopped, then said thoughtfully, "I guess that's one area where you two would agree. She doesn't think I belong here."

The platter of ribs made a loud clanking sound when Jake forcefully set it on the table. When she glanced up at him, her blue eyes widened in surprise. His face was set in a scowl, his jaw clenched tightly.

"I haven't said anything lately about you not belonging here," he pointed out in a gruff voice.

"No," she admitted slowly. "You haven't actually said it in the last few weeks. But you might as well say it." His eyes glittered dangerously. She continued in a quick rush. "Everytime I suggest even a small change at the office, you fight me tooth and nail. For example," she said in a firm voice, "you cancelled those signs I ordered without even trying them first."

He drew a deep breath. "So?"

"So, if you valued my opinion, you could have at least tried them."

Sitting down at the table, he began loading his plate. "I'll think about it."

Fighting back her irritation, she joined him. "Right," she said with patent disbelief.

At her tone, he looked up and met her gaze. Cor-

184 / LEANNE BANKS

rectly reading her frustration, he gave a half-smile and nodded at the challenge he saw in her eyes.

Fighting the electricity humming between them, Chelsea focused her attention on her meal. After an unproductive effort at using her knife and fork, she gave in and picked the succulent meat up with her fingers.

"What else did your mom have to say?"

Chelsea sighed. The letter had bothered her. Part of her wanted to dismiss it and part of her wanted to unburden herself. She was surprised Jake appeared interested. She gave a mental shrug. "She asked when I was going to come to my senses and come back to Richmond." Chelsea rolled her eyes and licked a finger. "Then she mentioned this man I used to date occasionally and what a wonderful husband he would make."

Chelsea glanced at Jake and noticed he'd stopped eating. He looked a little stunned.

Jake cleared his throat. "You're not engaged, are you?"

"Of course not," she said, appalled at his assumption. "What kind of person do you think I am? If I was engaged, I wouldn't—" she pointed at Jake, remembering the night they'd shared and felt her cheeks heat. Unwilling to finish that comment, she blurted out, "Well, I wouldn't be going to a pool party with Chris Preston on Saturday night." Chelsea could have cursed. Why on earth had she told Jake about her date with Chris?

Trying to get past her discomfort, she continued, "For that matter, if I were engaged to someone in

Richmond, it wouldn't make much sense for me to live in Arizona.'' She stabbed her fork into her potato salad. "My mother was particularly interested in my relationship with this man because of his family's political connections. My stepfather is running for office. So my mother, who is a frustrated politician, decided this would be a wonderful solution for everybody.''

"Why?"

"Well, my stepfather would receive the advantage of my fiancè's political connections. My mother would be included in a more socially elite circle. And I would have a wealthy husband." And Vivien would feel her years as a mother hadn't been an entire waste, Chelsea finished silently.

Jake sat very still, his face a mask. "Is that what you want, a wealthy husband?"

She wondered at his interest, considering the statement he'd made just over a week ago. Marriage isn't in my present or future. The words were engraved on her mind.

Glancing down at the plate of food, she felt her appetite suddenly wane. She set down her fork. "You must think I'm pretty shallow if you're asking me that question."

Avoiding his gaze, she wiped her hands and mouth with quick, jerky movements. "I just realized," she said struggling to keep her voice calm, "how tired I am."

She stood. "If you'll excuse me—"

His hand clamped over her wrist. "Don't go."

Unable to muster an appropriate response, she remained standing and gave a shaky laugh.

"Stay. I know you're not shallow. You're the sweetest person I know." His voice was low and husky.

Chelsea's head jerked up and her eyes searched his. He tugged gently on her wrist. She considered leaving. After all, his manner had almost crossed the line to insulting. But the light in his eyes drew her. He stood, towering over her with only the picnic table between them.

Without conscious thought, she leaned closer, mesmerized by his warm eyes. Jake bent toward her, his gaze intent on her mouth. Her eyelids fluttered. She was a breath away from Jake's kiss when Mozart nuzzled against Chelsea's free hand, whining for his share of the ribs.

Chelsea's eyes popped open. She jerked back, breaking the spell. Where was her mind? She had a nasty habit of leaving it on the shelf when she was with Jake. Clearing her throat, she pulled her wrist from his grasp. When she caught his glance, his eyes burned her like hot coals.

She looked away, focusing her attention on Mozart. "I bet you're hungry," she said to the dog. "You'll have to see if you can persuade Jake to share a few of the ribs."

Jake whistled and tossed a rib to Mozart. "Beggar," he said without vehemence. Then he sat down and looked at Chelsea as if he expected her to join him.

But she knew she should leave. It was useless to

see Jake even for a meal, when everytime she was with him she forgot there was no chance for love between them. At least he wasn't in love with her. "Thanks for the ribs. I'll leave both pieces of the cheesecake for you." She grabbed her glass and plate, hoping to leave quickly.

"Would your mother approve of Chris Preston?" He rasped out the question.

She stopped. The question had come out of nowhere. What did Jake care about her mother's opinion of anything? But he was waiting for an answer. Chelsea cocked her head to one side, considering the matter. "I guess she would. He's attractive. A sophisticated lawyer moving up." Chelsea shrugged.

"Is that why you're going out with him?" His tone was cynical, even condemning.

She resented his inference. "No. I'm not going out with him because my mother would approve."

He narrowed his eyes. "Then why are you going out with him?"

Her annoyance grew. "Not that it's any of your business," she said, "but Chris Preston is an attractive man who seems to appreciate my company. He values my opinion." Jake's face grew darker with each statement she made. But Chelsea's ego was still stinging from Jake's rejection of her. Heedless of his response, she continued. "He also doesn't have any hang-ups about my background."

She knew she was using Chris as a way to get back at Jake, but she was too hurt and angry to care. Snatching up her fork and gripping it as if it were a weapon, she gave a parting, completely unrelated shot. "And he doesn't smoke."

She turned to leave. Bowing to courtesy, she called over her shoulder, "Thank you for dinner." She barely resisted stomping off like a child. The blood roared in her ears such that she couldn't discern his low-voiced grumblings.

With the steam rising from his own ears, Jake watched her walk purposefully to the guest house. Although tempted to run after her and haul her back to his house, he restrained himself. He told himself it wouldn't do any good. She was still skittish of him, still hurt over the horrible way he'd hurt her and rightfully so.

And what would he tell her anyway, he asked himself. Jake threw another rib to Mozart and prowled restlessly around the picnic table, tossing trash into a bag. He balked at the notion of marriage. But the prospect of Chelsea attired in a skimpy bathing suit on a date with Chris Preston was enough to send Jake through the roof.

He could just imagine how she would look. His blood heated at the image of Chelsea lying in the sun wearing a bikini and an inviting smile. Chelsea and Chris Preston. Jake scowled. He reached for his cigarettes, remembering her taunt about his smoking. The hell with it. He never let a woman tell him what he could and couldn't do.

Jake lit a cigarette and drew deeply. The nicotine combined with his discontent, tasting bitter in his mouth. The image of Chelsea with another man nagged at him. Her feminine ego obviously needed stroking, and he didn't want Chris Preston doing the stroking.

She belonged to him.

The realization hit him with the force of a knockout punch. He belonged to her. They belonged together. Forever.

He sat down onto the picnic bench, allowing the implications of belonging to soak into his brain. His heart had already known, for a long time. Jake tried to remember when he hadn't felt this twisting in his gut over Chelsea.

Ed had shown him pictures of her, shared her letters with him. As a child, she'd charmed him. But when the pictures he'd seen had revealed a beautiful young woman, Jake had been beguiled. Although he'd never admitted it before, his inability to form a lasting relationship with another woman probably had its roots in his preoccupation with Chelsea Collins.

Jake shook his head and blew out another stream of smoke. It was crazy. He'd never even met her before she'd pranced her way into his warehouse, calmly informing him of her plans to be his business partner. He smiled at the memory.

At least she's not indifferent, he thought, making plans. There was only one solution. He'd marry her. It would take some scheming since she was still upset with him. But, as Ed had always told him, Jake Slater could achieve anything he set his mind to. And right now, Jake Slater's mind was set on Chelsea Collins.

Jake took one last draw on his cigarette. After dropping it to the dirt, he ground it out with his shoe.

He took the rest of the pack of cigarettes from his pocket and tossed them into the garbage bag. He'd buy some mints tomorrow.

Three days later, Chelsea dressed for her date with Chris. She attempted, with little success, to muster some enthusiasm for the date. As she arranged her hair into a French braid, she grimaced into the mirror.

What's wrong with you? she asked herself. Think of how attentive Chris is. He's called nearly every day this week. Think of how complimentary he's been. Think of how attractive and clever he is.

But try as she might, whenever Chelsea tried to picture Chris's handsome blonde features, a big man with dark hair and hot eyes invaded her mind. Memories of tender words murmured in his rough voice assailed her. Flashbacks of large hands oddly capable of touching her in gentle ways.

Chelsea groaned out loud in frustration when she saw the mess she'd made of her hair. She roughly untangled the blonde disarray, giving up on the braid and pulled it back into a simple ponytail.

It will get better, she assured herself. Once she moved into town with Anita, she would rarely see Jake. Pushing back the desolate feeling, she applied sunscreen to her face. She hadn't seen very much of Jake since the barbecue fiasco. And much to her annoyance, she'd looked for him. Everytime someone walked through the door at the office, she looked for him. Everytime she heard Mozart barking, she looked for him.

Mozart barked, and Chelsea heard the sound of a car motor running in the driveway. Her heart sped up, then settled back into a steady rhythm when she realized it was Chris. She secured the wispy cotton voile skirt and gave one last glance in the mirror.

She had to confess the outfit cheered her a little bit. The skirt was a mixture of pastel water colors coordinating with her peach tank swimsuit. The sales clerk had raved over how flattering the ensemble was to her coloring.

The doorbell rang. Shaking off her disturbing thoughts, she willed a pleasant smile to her face, grabbed her tote bag, and answered the door. "Hi, Chris. It's a great day for a pool party. Thanks for inviting me."

Chris's gaze fell over her appreciatively. "With an outfit like that, I'd say any day would be a great day for a pool party. You look lovely."

She pulled the door closed and locked it. "Why thank you. I found this outfit last week in Tucson."

Chris smiled and extended his arm. "It was worth the trip."

Chelsea smiled in return, then paused when she heard Jake's deep voice from behind her. "I agree." His gaze raked her from head to toe.

Her breath caught in her throat. She hadn't noticed his approach. Although Jake towered over both of them, he seemed to only have eyes for Chelsea. Swallowing, she said, "Jake and Chris, I'm sure you've met." Then she addressed Jake, "Chris and I were just on our way out."

Something about the way he looked at her made

her uneasy. She moved toward Chris's silver BMW. To her dismay, Jake walked along with them.

"So, you're going to a pool party?" Jake said it as if it was a question.

Chris shifted his dark sunglasses slightly. "Yes. My father's invited several of his friends. He wanted me to come." He touched Chelsea's bare shoulder. "I was fortunate to get written into Chelsea's social calendar, even though it took some work." Chris gave her a teasing grin. "She's been pretty busy."

"I guess so." Jake directed a pointed gaze to where Chris's hand rested casually on her shoulder. The young lawyer moved a little, allowing his hand to drop to his side. "How long are you going to be out?" Jake asked.

Chelsea's head jerked up. She watched his expression carefully. But he appeared cool and nonchalant, in a studied way. She narrowed her eyes; something wasn't right. Glancing at Chris, she noted he'd removed his sunglasses and was regarding Jake with a frown.

Linking her arm with Chris's, she stretched her lips into a reassuring smile. "Oh, don't bother with Jake. He has this misguided notion that he needs to look after me." She paused and gave extra emphasis to her next words, "In a big brother sort of way."

Chris could do nothing but smile in return as he led her to the passenger side of the car. Chelsea looked at Jake just before she slid into the car, taking in his forbidding expression. Normally, she would have been intimidated, but Chris's presence made her brave. Though she knew she might pay for it later, she said in a sweet voice, "Enjoy your evening, Jake. Don't bother waiting up."

She could practically hear his teeth viciously grinding his mints in response. Then she sank into the leather upholstery with a smile of deep satisfaction on her face.

It was a little after midnight when Chelsea slumped onto Anita Walker's guest room bed. "I really appreciate you letting me stay over tonight. Chris was so embarrassed when his car broke down. I think he felt even more humiliated when he couldn't figure out what was wrong with it."

Anita smirked and tossed Chelsea a nightshirt. "I'm sure Chris wouldn't have minded sharing his apartment with you."

Chelsea rolled her eyes. "I'll pass. Chris mentioned something about borrowing his father's car to take me home tomorrow." She sighed tiredly. "I guess he could have taken me home tonight."

Shaking her head, Anita gave Chelsea some linens. "It would have been at least another hour before you'd gotten home. It's much better for you to stay over here."

"It would have been late," Chelsea conceded, then stopped and groaned. "I wonder what Jake will have to say when he notices what time I show up."

Anita knitted her brow in confusion. "Why should he say anything? You keep telling me how he wants you to leave. I mean, it's not like you two have any sort of relationship." Anita paused and studied Chelsea carefully. "Do you?"

Chelsea looked away from Anita's curious gaze. She'd been unwilling to confide her feelings about Jake to anyone. And she felt uncomfortable with the notion right now. "Well," she said slowly. "Not really."

"Not really," Anita repeated skeptically.

"I'm sure Jake has no desire for a—" Chelsea faltered over the next words, "committed relationship with me."

"Uh huh," said Anita as she sat beside Chelsea. "But what about you?"

"It wouldn't work," she answered too quickly.

Anita stared at Chelsea as if she was an alien. "You mean to tell me that you've gone and flipped over stone face when you could have Chris Preston."

Chelsea had to resist the impulse to defend Jake. Then she could have kicked herself for the protective urge. If ever a man didn't need defending, it was Jake Slater. She didn't want to discuss the subject any more. "What I meant was that it wouldn't work between us, regardless of my feelings. As far as Chris Preston is concerned, I think he's a nice, attractive man. A friend."

"Yeah, well I don't think Chris wants to be your friend."

"I'm not interested in a romantic relationship right now," Chelsea stated, trying to persuade herself as much as Anita. She plumped her pillow.

"Uh huh." Anita's voice was heavy with disbelief.

"I'm not." Chelsea feigned a yawn. "But I am sleepy. It really is wonderful of you to let me have your guest bed on such short notice.'' She smiled. ''Thanks.''

Anita stood. ''Anytime. After all, you'll be moving in here soon. Good night, Chelsea.'' She gave an impish grin before she closed the door. ''And good luck with Jake.''

Chelsea opened her mouth to protest but Anita had already gone.

When she arrived home the next morning, Chelsea figured she could have used that good luck Anita had wished her the night before. She'd barely made it to her door before Jake showed up like a dark cloud ready to rain down its wrath on her.

''Where have you been?'' he demanded, following her into the guesthouse.

''To a pool party,'' she answered mildly and dumped her tote bag on a stool. She tried not to notice how attractive he looked in his canvas shorts and T-shirt.

''And after that?'' he gritted out, cornering her between the counter and himself.

She could feel the crinkly hairs on his muscular legs against her own nearly bare legs. He was frowning at her furiously, his stance purely male with his hands resting on his lean hips. Her knees weakened at his nearness. Crossing her arms over her chest, she shook her head at her wayward thoughts and replied in her most polite voice, ''That's not your concern, Jake.''

''The hell it isn't. Staying out all night.'' He waved his hand. ''Anything could have happened to you.''

"As you can see, nothing did."

When he shifted slightly, she made her escape, finding his proximity hazardous to her concentration. "Are you saying nothing happened between you and Chris Preston and you stayed out all night with him?"

The impact of what he was insinuating hit her all at once. Insulted, she saw red. "You've got a lot of nerve."

His face was tight. "You didn't answer my question."

She moved to the door and held it open. "You don't know me very well if you have to ask."

He looked uncertain, then determined. Walking to the door, he turned to her and said in a no-nonsense voice, "You shouldn't go out with Chris Preston any more. It'll ruin your reputation if he makes a habit of bringing you home the next morning. Everybody in town will be talking if they hear about it."

Incredulous, her eyes widened. "Reputation! This is the first time I've heard you express any concern for my reputation. Especially after . . . If you're so worried about my reputation, you should be thrilled that I'll be moving into town."

He took her response with infuriating calm and walked out the door. "Get rid of Preston, Chelsea."

Chelsea practically shrieked. Then she called to his back, "To coin your favorite phrase, forget it." Then she slammed the door.

She was breathless from the argument. Her face was hot. Her heart raced and her hands trembled. Chelsea expelled a long, shaky sigh. She'd been so determined to remain cool and calm when he grilled her about last night, but she'd lost it like she always did with him.

The man knew exactly which buttons to push with her. Whenever she was with him, she spent half her energy fighting her strong attraction to him and the other half trying to gather her wits enough to carry on a reasonable conversation. Chelsea groaned. As soon as he got back from his trip, she could move to Anita's. And though the prospect left her with a hollow, achy feeling, Chelsea faced the fact that she needed to get away from him.

Around midday on Monday she was writing up bidding information when Jake came up behind her. "You've done a good job," he said.

Caught off guard, she swung around and gaped at him. "Thank you," she managed over her surprise.

He nodded, then transferred his attention to the turquoise jumpsuit she wore. She held her breath when he touched the mandarin collar. "This is pretty," he said simply and caught her gaze.

Between his light touch and his compliments, Chelsea was left speechless. She simply stared in response, trying to remember when he'd been so outwardly approving of her.

Before she could muster a response, he gave her a knowing grin and said, "I'll see you later."

It had sounded like a promise. Hit and run, she thought. That's what she felt like. He'd hit her with those compliments and before she could figure out what was going on he'd run.

Over the course of the next few days, Jake visited

the office in the morning several times, often complimenting her on her work or the color of a blouse or piece of jewelry she wore. Everytime, she was completely befuddled and was hard pressed to come up with an intelligent response. This was so unlike him, except for that brief period after Father's Day.

The cigarettes were noticeably absent. He still patted his pockets as if searching for them, but instead he reached for mints. She'd started to ask him about his trip several times, but he always seemed to have an excuse about why he couldn't discuss it.

For herself, she was torn between wanting to stay and wanting to leave. But it was sheer torture for her to look out her window in the evenings to watch Jake and Mozart enjoy a game of fetch.

One such evening she stood staring out her window at him. The day had turned to night and Jake was feeding Mo. She admired his strong form and the gentle manner he had with the dog. Suddenly, he turned to face her. She froze. Surely he couldn't see her mooning over him, could he? Then Chelsea realized she'd left the light on. She groaned and moved away from the window.

Not one moment later, there was a light tap on her door. She opened it and her heart leapt into her throat. He leaned against the door frame wearing light cotton shorts and a yellow sport shirt that looked marvelous against his tan. His eyes traveled over her with masculine appreciation. He gave her a lazy grin that had a devastating effect on her pulse rate. "It's a nice evening."

"Um hmm," she murmured, when his eyes lingered on her lips.

"Why don't you come out for a walk?"

Why, she thought. There were only a thousand reasons why she shouldn't go for a walk with him. But she couldn't summon one of them to her mind when he looked at her that way. Uncertain, she hesitated.

He reached for her hand, enclosing it in the warmth of his own. "Come on," he urged, pulling gently. "You haven't seen enough of the desert at night."

Her heart twisted at the thought that she wouldn't be here in the guest house much longer to enjoy the unspoiled beauty of Jake's land. This could be a farewell. When her mind set off warning signals, she shrugged them off.

Chelsea gave a small smile, storing the sight of him in her mind—big and strong with that special light in his dark eyes. "Okay, show me your desert."

TEN

They walked silently for several moments, his rough hand gently enfolding her smaller one. She was acutely aware of his touch, his powerful stride modified to accommodate hers, his clean male scent.

A lovely breeze wafted over her skin. The sky was a sheen of black satin with glittering diamonds spread as far as the eye could see. She stopped and simply stared. "It seems so big."

Moving behind her, he rested his chin on the top of her head. "It is." His voice rumbled pleasantly next to her ear.

When she shivered at the sensation of his strong body against her back, he asked, "Are you cold?"

She stumbled out, "No." But he'd already wrapped his arms around her. She could have moved away. He wouldn't have prevented it. But he felt too warm and gentle.

"Part of the reason it seems so big is because there aren't any buildings to mar the horizon," he explained in a low voice.

It was strange how they both talked in hushed voices, as if they spoke too loudly the magic of the night would disappear. "It's beautiful."

"Yes," he said simply. Then he turned her so he could look at her face. "Tell me, Chelsea lady, after living on the east coast in the city for your whole life, what do you think of our desert?"

He'd asked the question almost playfully, but his eyes were serious. She thought it over. "At first, I thought it was barren, isolated, and lonely. I guess I've changed my mind. There's a peacefulness, a serenity here." She looked away from his intense gaze. "I'll miss it when I move in with Anita."

His arms tightened. Then he nuzzled her neck. "Mo will miss you."

"I'm glad someone will," she managed dryly.

When he laughed, she felt stupid so she started to pull away. But he only held her more securely. He bent his forehead down so that it touched hers. "Mo's not the only one who will miss you."

Then he kissed her, moving his warm mobile mouth over her pliant one. She didn't resist. Her mental processes came to a halt. She twined her hands up around his neck, fondling the hair on his nape.

He deepened the kiss, sliding his velvet tongue along her lips until she granted access. A fire ran through her veins, causing her to stretch closer, as close as she could get to him.

He moaned and kissed her jaw. "Why are you going out with Chris Preston when I'm the man you want?" he murmured.

For a moment, the meaning of the words didn't penetrate, she concentrated so fully on his touch. When they did, she stiffened, "Chris Preston?"

"You don't want him." His voice was silky, persuasive.

"But—"

Breaking off her objections, he kissed her again. She began to resist.

"It's not for you to say," she finally got out.

He sighed and aimed another kiss for her nose. "Yes, it is. You want me. You wouldn't be out here with me if you didn't."

Distressed, she shook her head and pushed at his chest. "No."

"Sure you do," he continued confidently. "You would have moved out of the guest house if you didn't."

She finally moved out of his arms. "But you said you were going out of town," she protested. "You asked me to watch Mo."

He looked a little uncomfortable when she mentioned that. Chelsea's stomach began to feel queasy. "You aren't going?"

He looked away, but his silence told her everything. Confused, she stumbled backward. "You lied to me."

Jake's head whipped back around. "Chelsea," he began

"No." She shook her head. "I don't want to hear

any more. You run hot, then cold. And I've never felt more humiliated than when you left me . . ." Her voice faltered.

She turned and ran. "Chelsea," Jake called, running after her. "You're overreacting. There's something you don't know."

He caught her arm and she jerked away. "Leave me alone." Her voice cracked.

"You're all upset for nothing."

Nothing. This was all nothing to him. Coldly, she repeated, "Leave me alone, Jake."

He wavered at her icy tone, his face showing uncertainty for the first time. He relented, but with a warning. "This isn't finished."

She didn't answer because she saw no need to argue over a fact of life. Chelsea rushed back to the guest house, the beauty of the evening lost to her.

She didn't know why he'd lied to her, but it obviously wasn't because he loved her. He'd had ample opportunity to express it and hadn't. The only other option she could see was that he'd changed his mind about having an affair with her.

Slamming the door closed, she stalked through the small house. It will be a cold day in hell, she thought, before she'd consent to an on-again, off-again affair with that Neanderthal.

Bursting with indignation, she pulled out her suitcases. Jake thought he had her right under his thumb. If she continued to live here, he could monitor and harass her dates and insinuate his way into her life. She was disgusted with her weakness toward him.

All he had to do was smile or put his arms around

her and she lost all her good sense. There was only one solution. She had to get away from him. Out of the guest house.

And this time it had to be for good.

Staring after her in the darkness, Jake expelled a steady stream of air from his lips. Women. Would they ever make sense? But only one needed to make sense to him. And he wanted her, even if he didn't understand her.

He'd been so confident of his approach this evening. The moon, stars, and soft breeze had cooperated with him. He'd caught her staring out her window at him. The timing had seemed perfect. She'd been warm and giving in his arms. Then everything fell apart.

He should have kept his mouth shut about Chris Preston. But that whole situation was driving him nuts. Preston was everything he wasn't. The fact that Chelsea had not only gone out with him but also ended up staying out all night sent his temperature through the roof.

Deep within, he *thought* she loved him. Kicking a clod of dirt, he looked at her house one last time. Jake walked to his house. She'd get over it. That was one thing he could count on from Chelsea. She might be a tad impulsive, but she didn't hold onto her anger. He'd give her some space and talk to her tomorrow night. Maybe flowers would help.

Chelsea stared into the bathroom mirror and frowned. Something still wasn't quite right. She added more blusher and paused. Perhaps a deeper color lipstick would take that wan look away. She carefully applied the crimson color to her lips.

"Damn!"

At this rate she'd have her entire collection of cosmetics painted, brushed, or smudged across her face. There was no beauty product that had been invented that could put the sparkle back into her sad eyes, or bring a happy glow to her skin, or make her strained smile appear genuine. Disgusted with herself, she capped the lipstick, threw it into her cosmetic bag, and flipped off the bathroom light.

Four days. It had been four lousy days since Chelsea packed up her belongings and moved into Anita's spare room. Anita had tactfully allowed her the space she'd needed without asking too many questions. Bless her, Chelsea thought, as she pulled on her sheer silk stockings.

She'd successfully avoided Jake by staying in the warehouse. There had been one or two close calls when he'd shown up for a surprise visit. The delivery of the signs she'd ordered had thrown her. But she tried not to read anything into it. She told herself she was doing the right thing, following the most sensible course of action.

So why was she so utterly miserable?

"Hey, Chelsea, are you almost ready? Chris and Paul should be here in five minutes," Anita called from her bedroom.

"Just about," she called back. After all her disdain over construction workers, Anita had met the recently hired carpenter and flipped. Paul was an attractive, good-humored young man who seemed to feel the same way about Anita. He claimed she was pretty special for him to put on a tux.

Chelsea could think of another man who would need a pretty special reason to put on formal evening attire. But she was confident she wouldn't see Jake tonight.

She pulled the figure-hugging white sheath over her head and adjusted the straight fold-over neckline that bared both of her shoulders. She pushed up the sleeves and smoothed the silky material over her hips, allowing the hem to slither to her feet.

The dress, with the way it encased her curves, was more daring than her usual taste. A shapely leg peeked from the side slit that ended just above her knee. Tossing her head with a touch of defiance, she decided she could use a little daring tonight.

The doorbell rang and she quickly attached her pearl drop earrings. She stepped into her high-heeled sandals, grabbed her purse, and left the bedroom with a resigned sigh.

Jake arrived during dessert.

Chelsea's fork fell to her plate with a loud clang while a piece of the chiffon cake went down the wrong way. She coughed repeatedly, her eyes filling with tears.

Chris patted her on her back. "Are you okay? Here, have some water." He held the water glass to her lips.

Swallowing her last coughs, she gave him a feeble smile and sipped from the glass. "Thank you."

"Anytime," he said and didn't remove his hand from her shoulder.

She'd hoped this date with Chris would distract her from her problems with Jake, but she was finding it increasingly difficult to keep Chris at arm's length as the evening wore on. After openly admiring her dress, he'd used every opportunity to touch her.

Shifting her chair, she moved far enough away that Chris had to remove his arm. She breathed a sigh of relief. Then she sneaked a surreptitious glance in Jake's direction. What was he doing here?

He sat in the back of the room, his gaze roaming the tables, as if he was searching for someone. Then his eyes locked on to hers and Chelsea thanked God she was sitting down, because her knees wouldn't have been able to support her. He stared with such purposeful intensity that she looked away.

She tried to focus her attention on Mayor Preston's speech, but she felt Jake's gaze like a touch. Several awards were presented to honor citizens who had contributed in a special way to the community center. To her surprise, Collins and Slater was called out for the last award of the evening. The mayor commended Jake for continuing the tradition Ed Collins had started of encouraging his employees' involvement in the center.

When the mayor finished, he waited expectantly for Jake to make his way to the front. Knowing her heart would be in her eyes if she looked at Jake right now, she kept her gaze trained on the podium at the front of the room. She started when she felt a warm, calloused hand on her shoulder.

She'd know that hand anywhere.

Turning slowly, she raised her questioning eyes to his. "You're a partner in this business," Jake said in a low voice. "You deserve the credit as much as I do. C'mon."

Chelsea shook her head. "No. I haven't been here that long. He didn't call out my name."

Her protests fell on deaf ears as Jake drew her from her seat. Wanting to avoid a scene, she finally relented and joined him at the podium.

Jake cleared his throat. "It's a lot easier to just continue on with what someone else started. Most of you who knew Ed Collins were aware of his contributions to the community." Jake grinned. "Many of you are probably still recovering from the arm twisting he was so famous for."

There were several nods and chuckles throughout the room. He still held her hand firmly, and Chelsea drank in the sight and sensation of closeness to him. He looked absolutely devastating in his tux. Like a wild animal allowing himself to be tamed for the moment, with the full realization that he could turn back to his primitive instincts in a blink of the eye.

Then he turned to her and she melted under his gaze. "At Collins and Slater, we're fortunate to be able to continue Ed Collins's traditions in more than one way. We have the legacy of his daughter. And though she's a lot easier on the eyes than Ed was . . ." There were a few guffaws and murmurs of agreement to that statement. Jake paused and Chelsea could feel the color rise to her cheeks. "Chelsea embodies the heart and soul of Ed Collins in such a way that it almost seems like he's still here."

Her heart overflowed at his words. Tears threatened and she blinked furiously to keep them from spilling onto her cheeks. Jake motioned for her to speak.

Taking a deep breath, she swallowed down the lump in her throat. "Thank you," she said. Her voice held a tremor. "For offering your friendship and love to my father, and now for opening your arms to welcome me." She shrugged, emotion brimming from her heart and eyes. "Thank you," she whispered. At that moment, Chelsea realized she'd succeeded in making a place for herself at Collins and Slater and in White Bluff.

The room erupted into applause. Jake's hand stretched firmly around her waist as they walked away. "We need to talk," he said in a low voice.

When he tried to lead her to the back of the room, she shook her head. "I'm here with Chris."

"So?" His face turned dark with disapproval.

Snapping out of her teary reverie, she responded, "So it would be rude to leave him."

She pulled away from him. He frowned and clenched his jaw. She could see the effort it cost him not to raise his voice. "We're not finished, Chelsea."

Her heart leapt at the way he said we. Then she recalled that he'd never professed his love to her. "Yes, we are," she said firmly.

Locking her wrist in his clasp, he growled in her ear, "I've been waiting for four days to clear up this mess and I'll be damned if I wait past tonight. You go make your excuses to Preston. I'll wait here.''

He released her and she walked swiftly to her seat beside Chris. Only she didn't make any excuses. Chelsea figured she'd have to be insane to join Jake in any conversation more controversial than the weather. By the menacing glint in his eye, she concluded that the weather was the furthermost thing from his mind.

So she tried to ignore him. A combo began playing music. She made her escape by joining Chris for a dance, followed by a turn around the floor with his father. After that, the faces became a blur. Her ankle began to throb and she'd just about decided to sit the next one out when Jake came to stand in front of her.

Her heart stopped, then pounded into a runaway rhythm. She considered fleeing, but he clasped her hand in his. "Shall we?"

Dreading the confrontation with all her being, Chelsea acquiesced. "Yes," she said, the one word oozing reluctance.

His arms eased around her, drawing her close to his warmth. It was a supreme combination of agony and ecstasy for Chelsea. The sensation of his hard chest against her breasts, his strong thighs against her, his hand firm at her waist all served to fill her mind and heart with images and emotions of other times when he had held her.

A shaky sigh escaped her lips. She dared one glance into his smoky eyes, then fastened her gaze onto his collar. They moved in a slow, circular shuffle.

"I want you back."

If her pulse raced any faster she was going to black out, she admonished herself. He didn't mean that the way it sounded. "Back where?"

"Back with me."

Her heart sank. If he wanted her back with him it was for only one reason. Chelsea shook her head, ignoring the possessive fire in his eyes. "We've tried that. It just won't work, Jake."

His jaw worked in frustration. "Why not?"

"We want different things," she explained, wishing she could leave. Her emotions were so close to the surface she feared she wouldn't be able to conceal the weakness she felt.

His eyes flashed with irritation. "I want you," he said bluntly.

Oh, God, she thought. He's going to give me a heart attack if I let him keep on. "It's no use, Jake. I'm not moving back to the guest house." She attempted futilely to pull her hand from his.

"Who said anything about the guest house?"

That stopped her. She stared at him. "Well, where else . . ." Then it dawned on her that he was suggesting she live in his house with him. Yet he hadn't mentioned marriage. A rage ripped through her veins. The anger roared in her ears. Her face must have revealed her fury because Jake watched her with a wary expression. She spoke in clipped tones. "If you think for one minute that I'm going to move in with you for a no-strings affair, then you can just—''

He cut her off with an incredulous, ''No-strings affair!'' Since he neglected to keep his voice lowered, they drew the attention of several other dancing couples. The onlookers watched them with curious eyes.

Chelsea's cheeks turned crimson. Jake glanced around, ''Aw, hell,'' he said vehemently. With an expression of total frustration, he hauled her up into his arms and strode to the door.

By this time, Chris Preston had noted the fact that his date for the evening was going to disappear if he didn't do something. ''Hey, Chelsea, what's going on?'' Chris chased after them.

She opened her mouth to speak, but Jake interrupted. ''Get your own woman, Preston. This one belongs to me.''

Chelsea struggled against him, pushing at his hard chest.

Chris protested, ''Now wait just a minute.''

But Jake only glared at him. ''I've waited as long as I'm going to. Now, if you'll excuse us, we've got a wedding to plan.''

Chelsea stopped pushing and stared at him, taking in his determined face. ''Wedding,'' she repeated weakly.

He turned his fiery gaze to her. ''Yes, wedding. And you'd better get used to the idea because I'm in no mood for a long engagement.'' Then he whisked through the door and headed for the parking lot.

She was still trying to comprehend his words. "Engagement?"

"Short engagement," he corrected gently, his eyes asking questions she thought he'd never ask her.

When he placed her in the jeep, she asked, "Jake, where are we going?"

He scooted into the driver's seat and fastened his seatbelt. "Somewhere we can talk privately, without any interruptions." He looked at her meaningfully and started the engine. "From your friends."

They spent the rest of the drive in silence with Chelsea's mind going a million miles a minute. He wanted to marry her. That's what he'd said. But the absence of the three words that were so important to her hung over her like a dark cloud.

He'd barely stopped the jeep before grabbing her wrist and pulling her out the door. Her dress and sandals hadn't been designed for running. She stumbled in her efforts to keep up with him. "Wait, I can't go this fast in this dress."

He paused, sidetracked, when he stared down at the dress. "That oughta be illegal," he muttered and picked her up in his arms. "I don't want you wearing that dress in public again."

She didn't like his presumptuous tone, but she was learning his gruffness often hid vulnerability. "You don't like it?"

"Sure, I like it," he growled, pushing open the door to his house. "Any red-blooded man who isn't blind would like it. That's the problem."

After setting her down on the couch, he pulled off his jacket and undid his bow tie along with a few of the top buttons to his shirt. Chelsea swallowed at the sight of him. He was so irresistibly masculine.

And she was so susceptible to him.

A quiver of fear ran through her. What if, after all this, he still couldn't say he loved her? Were the words so important, her heart asked. Yes, they were. Chelsea looked up at him.

He prowled around the room restlessly and poured himself a drink. Now that he had her undivided attention, he seemed strangely reluctant to talk. He cleared his throat. "Do you want something to drink?"

Her mouth dry with nervousness, she shook her head.

"Something to eat?"

She shook her head again.

He took a deep breath as if fortifying himself and sat beside her. For once in her life, she couldn't think of a way to fill the silence. So she waited while he took several swallows from his glass of Scotch. The silence seemed to go on forever.

Finally, he set the glass on the end table and turned to her. His hungry gaze lingered on her bare shoulders. "You look pretty." He reached out to run a rough thumb along her collar bone.

The touch sent a shiver through her. He felt the tiny movement and looked into her eyes. "So, will you?"

She wasn't leaving anything to chance with this man. There'd been too many misunderstandings in the past. "Will I what?"

"Marry me," he answered in a husky voice, his gaze searing her with its intensity.

Yes, she wanted to scream. Instead, she looked away and asked a question of her own. "Why? Why do you want to marry me, Jake?"

He muttered a curse under his breath and stood. "Well, hell, Chelsea, why do you think I want to marry you?" He jammed his hands into his pockets and began to pace. "I can't get you out of my head, no matter what I'm doing. I'm not worth a flip at work. I can't sleep." He looked uncomfortable. "And when I do sleep, I end up dreaming about you."

"So you want to marry me so you can get back to work and get some sleep?" she asked.

"No!" Jake expelled a heavy sigh. "Lord, I'm botching this." He turned around and sat back down beside her. "I've never asked a woman to marry me before." He touched her chin, gently guiding her to face him. "Chelsea, lady-love, look at me. Give me some hope. I'm practically dying with love for you and all you can do is ask questions."

Her heart jumped into her throat. Her head snapped up. "Say that again," she whispered.

He frowned. "All you can do—"

"No," she interrupted. "That you love me."

Instantly, he comprehended. His voice was husky. "I love you."

She dove into his arms which held her tightly to him. "Is that all I had to say? But you must have known."

"I didn't." The denial was muffled against his

chest. "After the night you left me—" Her voice cracked with emotion. Even now, she still felt the remembered pain.

Jake tightened his arms. "Oh, you'll never know how I suffered over how I treated you that night. I swear I'll make it up to you. I'll never leave you again."

Urging her head upward, he planted nuzzling kisses along her jaw and cheek. He reached her lips, swallowing her sigh of pleasure into his mouth. Her eyes filled with tears at the sweetness and commitment in the kiss. Without reserve, she kissed him back, relishing the sensation of his masculine body pressed to her feminine form.

He pulled away slightly, with strong breaths. "You still haven't answered my question," he said in a husky voice.

Still reeling from their kiss, Chelsea frowned in confusion. "What?" Then her lips tilted into a smile of understanding. "Yes," she said and watched his smile reflect her own.

He pulled her onto his lap and his face grew solemn. "That night we made love, you scared the hell out of me."

Surprise flooded her. "Scared you."

Jake nodded. "You see, I've never really had anybody that belonged to me. My dad left when I was little. Then my mother got sick and died. Ed was the closest thing to a father I ever had, and I was lucky to have him. But I never really belonged to him either. And then he died." He hesitated. "There have been a few women. But when you get used to depending on yourself, it's hard to open up to other people. Everything changed when you came.''

Jake stared at Chelsea in wonder. ''You walked into my life, batted your eyelashes, and stole my heart. I just didn't know how to handle it, Chelsea. I still don't. And I couldn't believe it when you gave yourself to *me*. Me. The guy with more rough edges than a lumberyard.''

''Oh, Jake,'' Chelsea murmured with a full heart. ''You weren't that bad.''

He raised an eyebrow.

''You weren't,'' she insisted. ''Remember when you took care of me after my black eye and the spider bite. And how you hauled me off to your house when Father's Day came.'' She grimaced. ''You have been tough to work with. But I stuck it out, and I think it's made me stronger.''

Jake wrapped his arms around her. ''You were always strong. You just didn't know it. And God knows I'm the luckiest man alive to have you.'' He pulled away slightly and his voice became more ardent. ''I want to make you happy, but I'm new at this. I'm not used to depending on anyone else. Something tells me it probably takes a lot of practice.''

Chelsea smiled at the warning note in his voice. ''I hear married people practice many things, Jake.'' She kissed him softly and watched his eyes darken with emotion. ''When you get tired of practicing depending on me, I guess we'll just have to practice something else.''

When Jake started to kiss her again, she ducked

her head. Laughing at his consternation, she continued, "I have one more question."

Jake groaned.

"You drew that picture of me that's hanging on your bedroom wall, didn't you?"

He eased back, running his hands through her silky hair. "Yeah, I copied one of your dad's favorite pictures of you as a birthday present a few years ago. I figured it was a great idea. And Ed was so hard to buy for." Giving her hair a little tweak, he glared at her playfully. "I didn't count on getting so attached to it. I almost didn't give it to your father. He must have known. Ed gave it back to me when he went to the hospital for the last time."

Thoughtfully, Chelsea traced her finger on his bottom lip. "Do you think he could have known that we would fall in love?"

Jake gently captured her caressing finger between his teeth, then released it. Her heart beat faster at the hot sparks in his eyes. "I don't know. But I think he would have approved."

"I do, too," she whispered. She ran her hands down his neck and shoulders. Then she placed her palm inside his shirt, feeling the heavy pounding of his heart. "I love you, Jake. I want to marry you and have your children."

His big body shuddered. He gazed at her with such love she could have wept with joy.

Then he did what he'd been wanting to do for the past five minutes. He kissed her. Then they taught each other the ways and words of love.

*   *   *

Exactly one week later, Chelsea found herself once again being carried by Jake, this time into their honeymoon suite at the shore. When he'd asked her where she'd like to go, she confessed the beach was one thing she'd found missing in Arizona. Jake had promptly made reservations at a secluded beach off the coast of California.

"Jake, this is getting to be a habit," Chelsea chided her new husband.

"Are you complaining?" He dumped her onto the bed with the bouquet of roses he'd given her and began to unbutton his shirt.

"No." Chelsea smiled and kicked off her shoes. She went to the window and opened it, breathing in the fresh, salt air. The last week had been spent in a whirlwind of activity. Between getting blood tests, a marriage license, and shopping for a white dress, Chelsea had been deluged with bridal preparations. She and Jake had had little time to be alone with each other, and she found she was dying for some time with her new husband.

The wedding had been small with just their close friends in attendance. Al Walker and his wife, along with Anita and Butch. Her mother had sent her regrets with best wishes. Chelsea had been thankful for even that small concession.

Jake came up behind her, wrapping his arms around her. He turned her around and began to kiss her first gently, then sensuously. Chelsea grew warm and languid.

"Aren't you going to go let me change into my negligee?"

"What for?" he grumbled. "You wouldn't have it on for more than a few seconds."

She felt her cheeks heat. Jake watched the rosy color and chuckled. He pulled her back over to the bed. "C'mon, my shy little bride. I've got a present for you."

"Present?" she asked, sinking down onto the king-size mattress. "But you've already given me this gorgeous diamond." Chelsea held up her hand and admired the sparkling solitaire.

Then she gazed up at Jake. He'd removed the shirt, leaving his muscular chest exposed. She switched both her attention and admiration to her husband's attractive, masculine form. Her fingers itched to trace the muscles of his chest and abdomen.

Jake seemed to read her thoughts and his gaze grew sensual. "In a minute," he promised.

Jake reached into his pocket and drew out her father's gold watch. Jake's watch, she corrected herself. More than ever, she felt it belonged to him.

He clenched it in his hand, then held it out to her. "This is my most prized possession. Since you're more important to me than anything in the world, I thought you should have it."

Her heart turned over. Chelsea raised astonished eyes to him. She knew how much the watch meant to him. She also knew how much the gesture he was trying to make would cost him.

Raising up on her knees, she took his hand and closed it over the watch. "I can't let you do that, Jake."

He knitted his eyebrows in confusion. "But I

wanted you to have something that would prove how important you are to me.''

He was so intense and serious. So eager to assure her of his love. Too tense for their honeymoon, she thought, feeling concerned.

Her earlier self-consciousness faded in the face of her consuming love for Jake. She thought of how she could help him relax and smiled broadly.

Her lips feathered a kiss on his very determined chin. A gratifying ripple went through his powerful frame.

She burrowed her hands in the dark mat of his chest and was surprised she could feel the thud of his heart over the pounding of her own.

She dropped a warm kiss on his lips and watched his eyes grow hotter with every move she made. His possessive gaze absorbed her as he unfastened every button of her blouse and pushed it from her shoulders.

Her mouth went dry. Then she brushed her lips against his ear. He twitched at the tickling sensation of her soft breath. ''I don't want the watch, darling.''

His restraint tested, he hauled her flush against his chest. ''Then what do you want?'' His question was delivered in a rough rasp that raced along her sensitized nerve endings.

She gave him a smile of invitation issued exclusively to him. The power she held over this big man humbled her.

Pointing a pink-tinted fingernail at his chest, she simply said, ''Just you, Jake. Just you.''

SHARE THE FUN . . .
SHARE YOUR NEW-FOUND TREASURE!!

You don't want to let your new books out of your sight? That's okay. Your friends can get their own. Order below.

No. 57 BACK IN HIS ARMS by Becky Barker
Fate takes over when Tara shows up on Rand's doorstep again.

No. 58 SWEET SEDUCTION by Allie Jordan
Libby wages war on Will—she'll win his love yet!

No. 59 13 DAYS OF LUCK by Lacey Dancer
Author Pippa Weldon finds her real-life hero in Joshua Luck.

No. 60 SARA'S ANGEL by Sharon Sala
Sara *must* get to Hawk. He's the only one who can help.

No. 61 HOME FIELD ADVANTAGE by Janice Bartlett
Marian shows John there is more to life than just professional sports.

No. 62 FOR SERVICES RENDERED by Ann Patrick
Nick's life is in perfect order until he meets Claire!

No. 63 WHERE THERE'S A WILL by Leanne Banks
Chelsea goes toe-to-toe with her new, unhappy business partner.

No. 64 YESTERDAY'S FANTASY by Pamela Macaluso
Melissa always had a crush on Morgan. Maybe dreams do come true!

Kismet Romances
Dept. 1091, P. O. Box 41820, Philadelphia, PA 19101-9828

Please send the books I've indicated below. Check or money order only—no cash, stamps or C.O.D.s (PA residents, add 6% sales tax). I am enclosing $2.95 plus 75¢ handling fee for *each* book ordered.

Total Amount Enclosed: $_____.

____ No. 26	____ No. 38	____ No. 50	____ No. 59
____ No. 28	____ No. 40	____ No. 52	____ No. 60
____ No. 30	____ No. 42	____ No. 54	____ No. 61
____ No. 32	____ No. 44	____ No. 56	____ No. 62
____ No. 34	____ No. 46	____ No. 57	____ No. 63
____ No. 36	____ No. 48	____ No. 58	____ No. 64

Please Print:
Name _____
Address _____ Apt. No. _____
City/State _____ Zip _____

Allow four to six weeks for delivery. Quantities limited.